ALLEL KHEROUFI

I want to fly

A PLAY
FOR CHILDREN
IN FOUR PARTS

outskirtspress

DENVER, COLORADO

Dedication

To my daughter, Amanda, who did not get a chance to even dream about flying — she flew before her time. She flew like an angel to heaven, leaving her mother and me gazing at the sky, looking for unseen angels flying in blue skies full of bright stars.

I Want to Fly!

A four-part adventure about a duckling's dream to fly, and his determination to make that dream come true.

Foreword

To dream is to fly, and to fly is to dream; thus, every child has the ability to fly; and it makes a difference if that child has a desire to fly — but wait a minute! Flying implies arriving at a destination.

All children have dreams about what they want to be when they grow up, and with the help of their loving parents, they can achieve their goals. Just dreaming about it, however, is not enough. Achieving one's goal requires much dedication and a lot of hard work. And that's what this four-part play is about!

In Part I, our hero Homer Duck takes the first step towards achieving his goal: he has a dream to fly to the sun! In trying to reach that goal, Homer runs into all kinds of obstacles. Nothing seems to be in his favour, but he refuses to give up. He remains steadfast in his belief in himself, and that he can actually get what he sets his mind on. His mother, like many parents, has taught him not to give up on a dream but to persevere, because if he gives up on his dream he will have given up on his future. Without a future, what good is a dream?

What can parents do to encourage their children to pursue their dreams? Do you wish them success, or do you wish them luck? Wishes come from everyone; luck may come once in a lifetime, and not to everyone. It is the duty of all parents to instill in their children the courage to face whatever difficulty may arise, and to overcome whatever obstacle appears in the way.

I wish for all parents to see their children's dreams come true.

I wish for all children to fly above their obstacles and achieve their dreams.

I wish for all children to fly together to make this a beautiful planet to live on.

I wish for every child's dream to come true.

I wish for all parents to survive their children's dreams.

I wish for my son, Dean, to fly and to achieve his dream one day.

Allel Kheroufi

Part One

A Duckling's Dream

Our story begins at Lake Serenity. It is a quiet, peaceful lake surrounded by a pleasant forest. It is a beautiful spot to live in peace forever. Homer Duck lives here with his mother, Mathilda. Homer has one ambition: he wants to fly!

One evening in springtime, as Homer wanders by the lake's edge, he sees the sun's reflection in the water and marvels at this beautiful wonder. He dreams of the possibility of some day actually being able to fly to the sun and to touch it.

The next day, Homer leaves Lake Serenity, looking for the road that will take him to the sun. Soon, he wanders into the Kingdom of Barnyardia, where he meets King Mortimer and Queen Hortense, Lucy Goose and Henrietta Chicken and their families, and Sylvester Cat, the king's servant and chief advisor.

When Homer suddenly arrives in the Kingdom of Barnyardia, a complete stranger, and begins to talk of even stranger dreams of flying to the sun, everyone gets quite upset at such outlandish foolishness. How can a puny duckling with tiny wings and almost no real feathers possibly fly even a few feet? All the citizens of Barnyardia laugh at such silly dreams, but Homer is not deterred. He believes in himself, and is determined to find a way to fly to the sun.

Will Homer eventually get his dream to come true? How will he overcome the obstacles he will meet on the way? You can find the answers to these questions by reading this four-part adventure of a determined duckling.

Here is Part I —

A Duckling's Dream

The Characters

Homer	a duckling
Mathilda	a duck, Homer's mother
Sylvester	a cat, king's servant and advisor
King Mortimer	a turkey tom, king of Barnyardia
Queen Hortense	a turkey hen
Chanticleer	a rooster, a retired king
Henrietta	a hen
Jeremiah	a young cockerel
Penelope	a pullet
Lucy	a mother goose
Bartholomew	male gosling
Prunella	a female gosling
Nigel	a male pigeon
Priscilla	a female pigeon

The Setting

The Kingdom of Barnyardia, one late spring day.

Prologue

The scene is the edge of Lake Serenity, a very quiet, peaceful lake with clear blue water. It is surrounded by a wilderness forest. Birds fly above the water, meandering lazily in the air. It is evening, and the sky is clear. The sun at the edge of the water seems to just touch the water. Everything is peaceful. Homer appears by the water's edge. He gazes at the water and at the sun's reflection there in amazement.

Homer (loudly): Mother! Mother! Come quickly! What is this? It seems to be sinking into the water. It's going deeper and deeper.

Mathilda (somewhere in the background): Oh, it's probably nothing to worry about. Maybe it's just an unusual fish.

Homer (persistently): It's really amazing. I've never seen anything like it before.

Mathilda (still in the distance): Oh, don't worry yourself. Come on. It will soon be dark. We have to be getting home.

Homer (still gazing at the water as if hypnotized): It's moving! It's round, and it's coming towards me, towards my feet. Mother, I'm going to jump in and catch it!

> As the duckling prepares to dive into the water, the Mother Duck rushes forward to stop her foolish child.

Mathilda (fearfully): Stop! Don't jump in there!

> She quickly reaches the duckling's side and pulls it back to safety.

Homer: But Mother, I only wanted to get a good look at it.

Mathilda: Then we'll look at it together. Maybe it's some kind of dangerous fish!

> They both peer down into the water at the sun's reflection.

Homer (almost sobbing): See, it's almost gone. It's moving so fast.

Mathilda (laughing): Oh, my sweet young thing. You must be tired. Look at the sky. See? It's the sun setting. Here in the water, it's only the sun's reflection that you see. Look, the sun has already set. It's gone to bed. No sun in the sky, and no sun in the water. (They both look at the water.) Come, it's bedtime for the sun and for you. I'll tell you a wonderful bedtime story tonight.

> They exit. The sun sets slowly. The birds make their evening calls quietly as they settle for the night. The sky is still red, and slowly darkens. It is night.

ACT ONE
Scene One

Kingdom of Barnyardia at the edge of a forest. It is daybreak of a late spring or early summer day. From time to time the sounds of insects are heard. As the sun rises, it throws its light across the countryside. The hills, valleys, and trees take shape. Birds fly lazily in the air. In the foreground is the Royal Castle of Barnyardia; nearby is an old tree with many branches. Chanticleer gets up from his perch on one of those branches, finds an appropriate spot, stretches, flaps his wings, and crows his morning wake-up call three times. As he settles himself back on his perch again, Homer's singing voice is heard, coming from somewhere within the forest.

Homer (singing):
   The morning dawn is breaking; how beautiful is the sun.
   Its golden rays are quaking; how wonderful is the sun.
   It makes me feel so nice and warm; how gentle is the sun.
   I cannot come to any harm, how lovely is the sun. ...

   (He stops abruptly.) MOTHER? ! ? !!

   The sun is a golden globe suspended between the sky and the earth. The sky is clear, and the land shimmers in the morning light. Sylvester lies comfortably napping beside the castle wall, while in the tree, Chanticleer is catching forty winks after his ordeal of waking up the kingdom. Nigel and Priscilla enter joyfully singing and dancing.

Nigel and Priscilla (singing together):
   How beautiful we are,
      how wonderful the day.

We are happy little birds
    with bright, shiny feathers.
We fly here and there
    with no cares in the world.
How beautiful we are,
    how wonderful the day.

> Homer emerges from the forest and approaches the castle. He looks around perplexed, wondering how he got here. He spies Nigel and Priscilla just as they see him. All three are startled and jump with fright.

Nigel (in a quaking voice): Careful! It may be Sylvester, the Cat, in disguise.

Priscilla: No, it's not Sylvester. It looks like a baby bird of some kind.

Homer: Where am I? How did I get here? (Looking around in panic, looking for a way out.) Which way do I go? How do I get out of here?

> Nigel and Priscilla continue to watch Homer carefully from a distance.

Nigel: The poor thing is shaking.

Priscilla: Do you think maybe it's cold?

Nigel: Maybe it's hungry.

Priscilla (sneering): Look at it. It's naked. Almost no feathers. (She looks admiringly at her own beautiful plumage, then looks at Homer again and begins to laugh out loud. She continues teasing.) Poor little Birdie. (She takes a step towards Homer.) How come you have no feathers, Little Birdie?

Nigel: Leave him alone! Can't you see he's scared. Let's find him something to eat. Maybe that will cheer him up.

They approach Homer and make as if to pick him up to carry him off.

Homer (angrily): Leave me alone! Please leave me alone! All I want is to continue my path. Oh, how can I get away from here? (He looks at the sun.) How gentle and warm the sun feels. Just leave me alone to enjoy its pleasant rays.

By this time, Sylvester, the Cat, is awake and watches what is going on. Nigel and Priscilla spy him as he begins to move and stretch.

Nigel (with a worried look): It's Sylvester! He'll get the little Birdie.

Priscilla: What can we do to protect him from Sylvester?

Nigel: Let's take him with us.

As Nigel and Priscilla approach Homer, Sylvester jumps forward, frightening Nigel and Priscilla, who immediately run away, with Sylvester in pursuit.

Homer (very frightened): Mother! Mother! Where are you?

Homer runs back and forth, looking for a possible path that will lead him away from this place. Suddenly Sylvester returns.

Sylvester (authoritatively): Look here, You! Who are you? How did you get here? Where did you come from? What are you doing here, anyway?

Homer attempts to climb the tree.

Homer (tearfully): Mother! Mother! Where are you?

Sylvester jumps up and grabs Homer, bringing him down to earth.

Sylvester (angrily): Come on! (He holds Homer closer to him.) Tell me how you got here. How did you find your way to Barnyardia through the forest and the maze of pathways leading here?

Homer (very frightened): Please let me go. Just show me how to get out of here, and I'll never bother you again. I hate this dreadful place.

Sylvester (somewhat astonished): How can you say this place is dreadful and that you hate it? Barnyardia is the most beautiful place in the universe. (He turns suddenly, changing the subject.) I need a glass of milk. (He begins to walk away.) But before I go I have to know how you got here! (He pauses to think, scratching his head. He turns accusingly to Homer.) ... I've got it. ... You used magic to get here! You're a magician or a witch! I think you flew here on your broom. Where is it, eh? Where did you hide your broom?

> During this interrogation, Homer is totally perplexed. He doesn't know what to say. Indeed, he doesn't really have a chance to say anything. Finally, when Sylvester stops long enough, Homer sees his opening.

Homer (desperately): Yes! Yes! I want to fly!

Sylvester (not hearing a word Homer said): I want some answers now! How did you get here so easily? You didn't fly here ... did You? H-m-m?

Homer (sadly): I — want — to ...

Sylvester (again not hearing a thing): So, maybe you dragged yourself here on your belly like a snake. (He laughs derisively.)

Homer (angrily, and more loudly): I want to get away from here! I WANT TO FLY!

Sylvester (suddenly aware of Homer's words): What's that? What did you say? You want to fly? Now listen here! Do you know what would happen if everyone in Barnyardia wanted to fly?

Homer: I don't care about Barnyardia. All **I** know is that I want to fly.

Sylvester (sarcastically): How can you fly?

Homer: All I know is that my mother told me if I really wanted to fly, then I could fly.

Sylvester: No, no. It's not possible for you to fly.

Homer: But my mother says that anything in life is possible if you're determined enough to work hard for it.

Sylvester (very determinedly): I said you can't fly! That's all there is to it!

Homer: And why not? Why can't I fly?

Sylvester (uncertain of the answer): Because … because you … because you don't have enough feathers. — That's it. You don't have enough feathers. And … and you're not strong enough. Right! … You don't have enough feathers, and you're not strong enough. That's why you can't fly.

Homer (looking sadly at himself): Mother told me we were related to the White Storks.

Sylvester (laughing in disbelief): What? You? You're related to the White Storks? Do you really want to be related to them? (He inspects Homer carefully.) Well, let's take a look at you. H-m-m. Maybe at first glance, you do seem to have some stork-like qualities. Your wings seem strong enough, and they are covered with feathers. (Laughs again.) Maybe you **can** fly high — and for a long distance.

But, seriously, listen to me. Just stop this silly wishful thinking about flying, and don't bother anyone with your stupid ideas. If you want to live peacefully here with us, you have to live by our rules.

Here is how things work around Barnyardia. The two most prominent families are the Geese and the Chickens. They are superior to the rest of us. If they hear about your wish to fly, you'll be in big trouble. So just be quiet, and be happy with what you've got. (Whispers.) By the way, I can help you, if you let me. I have some influence in Barnyardia.

Now, as for the Turkeys, we can expect just about anything from them. Especially from King Mortimer. In other words, don't anger the King. He is very powerful, and some say he even has magical powers. So don't cross him!

Homer: Oh, do you have a king?

Sylvester (hesitantly): Yes. … We have … a king. …

Homer: Oh, good. Where is he?

Sylvester (still not sure he should be giving out this information): He … uh … went for … his … daily walk … with the Queen. (As if he suddenly remembered something important.) Oh, yes! I'm the Royal Chef. They will be back soon. I have to prepare lunch for them. (He looks at the sun.) It's almost noon. I have to go now.

Homer (blocking Sylvester's way): Can I speak with your king?

Sylvester (pushing Homer out of the way): No way! You can't talk to the King! First of all, you have to talk to me and get my permission, and then …

Homer (interrupting): Wait a minute. Are you saying that you have the power to do anything you want?

Sylvester (nervously): No, no, not me. Only King Mortimer can do anything he wants. He even decides who can live here and who can't.

Homer: But I'm not asking to live here.

Sylvester (laughing nervously): Do you think it's easy to be accepted here, and to live forever among these families? (He pauses.) ... I must go prepare lunch.

Homer (blocking Sylvester again): If the King agrees to help me, maybe I could fly!

Sylvester: You must understand. ... Listen carefully. King Mortimer can do anything he pleases; but, he can't make the decision by himself. I, too, have some influence and authority here in Barnyardia.

Homer (pausing to think): Just a minute. ... Are you saying? — Oh, I get it! You, Sylvester Cat, govern one-half of Barnyardia, and King Mortimer Turkey governs the other half. Is that it?

Sylvester (loudly): I said King Mortimer is the King of Barnyardia. (Whispering.) Don't say that again. Someone may hear you.

He looks up into the tree and points to Chanticleer, the rooster.

Homer (surprised): Oh, so you lied to me. The King is right here!

Sylvester quickly puts his paw to Homer's mouth.

Sylvester: Hush! Be quiet! This isn't the King. This is old Chanticleer, the former king. If he heard what you just said, he'd tell King Mortimer, and you'd be banished from Barnyardia.

Homer: I don't care. I don't want to stay here. I just want to find my way out of here and learn to fly.

Sylvester (sighing): And I need a glass of milk.

He goes behind the castle, and Homer sits on a fallen tree trunk. Nigel and Priscilla return.

Nigel (whispering): He's still here.

Priscilla: Yes. We have to do something to save his life before Sylvester gets back.

> The two approach Homer.

Nigel (gently): Come with us. We'll take you to a beautiful lake, where the water is clear and as blue as the sky. It's surrounded by tall green grass. You'll like it there.

> Sylvester is seen in the background slinking behind a tree, watching slyly.

Priscilla (somewhat agitated): You're not safe here. Hurry! Come with us!

> Sylvester jumps from behind the tree and chases Nigel and Priscilla.

Homer (frightened): Mother! Mother! Where are you? Help me!

> Sylvester returns, holding some pigeon feathers in his paws.

Sylvester (angrily): I missed them, but just wait. Sooner or later I'll get them. Then I'll have a good feed. (He turns to Homer.) Listen, you! Let's make a deal. You help me catch the pigeons, and I'll help you with King Mortimer.

Homer: If you really want to help me, show me how to get out of here.

Sylvester: You'll never get out of here by yourself. You need my help. You better help me catch those two pigeons, or you'll have real big trouble with the King.

Homer (pleading): Please! Please let me go.

Sylvester: Okay! But on one condition. (He gives Homer a trap.) Here, help me trap the pigeons, and I'll ask King Mortimer to give you anything you want.

Homer (nervously): You're not very nice!

Sylvester: Maybe not, but I am the Royal Chef, and the King's right hand. And that makes me powerful in Barnyardia. (He begins to sing):
I am the most powerful Chef.
— Anytime, … anywhere, …
I am the powerful Chef. No more — no less,
And everyone knows that I am the best.
My name is repeated by every mouth,
My wisdom is heard both north and south,
For I am the powerful Chef.
My presence causes teeth to chatter,
My absence makes the dishes clatter,
For I am the powerful Chef.

> He finishes singing and nestles himself by the castle wall.

Homer: You're useless.

Sylvester (oblivious to Homer's remark): I'm dreaming of a large bowl of nice warm cream.

> He stretches out lazily, closing his eyes.

Homer (angrily): All you can think of is food and filling your belly! You're disgusting.

Sylvester: Ah! This is the real life! I'm not a dreamer like you are.

Homer: I don't want to live like you do. You're a glutton!

Sylvester (jumping up angrily): What's that? What did you say?

Homer (a little bit scared): Oh, nothing. I was just thinking about flying.

Sylvester: And I said stop dreaming foolishly! You have to think about the real world and what you're going to do when you grow up!

> Meanwhile, Chanticleer, who has been sleeping, awakens and flaps his wings.

Homer (surprised): Who's that? Is that King Mortimer?

>   Chanticleer hops down and struts about. Sylvester gets up and saunters over.

Sylvester: Nah! That's nobody. It's only old Chanticleer. He's harmless.

Chanticleer (looks at Homer): What's this? (He comes closer to Homer and sniffs.) Yuck! What a foul smell! (He holds his beak.) I swear, I don't believe that a single drop of water has ever touched your body since you were born! You stink! Who are you? What are you doing here? What do you want from us?

Sylvester (sarcastically): He wants to fly!

Chanticleer: What! With those puny wings?

Sylvester: Yes, and not just a little flight. A long one, and high up into the sky!

Chanticleer: Well, that's utterly foolish! And so is he!

Homer: No, I'm not foolish! My mother told me I was smart enough to do whatever I set my mind to.

Chanticleer: Well, I bet you're not smarter than my little Sweeties!

Homer: And who are your Sweeties?

Sylvester: He means his family — the Chickens.

Chanticleer: Yes, I mean my family. Nobody in Barnyardia can fly higher than the Chickens. And nobody has brighter or more colourful wings than Jeremiah and Penelope, my little chicks.

>   Chanticleer gives Homer a push, and Sylvester steps between them.

Sylvester (to Chanticleer): I'm warning you. Leave him alone with his dreams. Just look at yourself. You never flew higher than a garbage can. You crow just to disturb our dreams with your abrasive voice in the mornings.

Chanticleer (somewhat taken aback by this tirade): You don't really know me or anything about my past. I was once a powerful king here in Barnyardia.

Sylvester: Your past means nothing now. This is the present.

Chanticleer: My grandmother once told me that her great-grandmother used to fly higher than this tree. (He points to the tree.) But now … I guess my time is over. But I still remember the good old days when I was king.

> He preens himself and begins to sing:

Barnyardia! O Barnyardia! My only love, Barnyardia.
Once upon a time, Barnyardia was my kingdom.
Once upon a time, I was king of Barnyardia.
Barnyardia, my love, my life. Barnyardia, my native land.

> As he finishes singing, he slumps to the ground. Homer comes over to help him up.

Homer: How many kings live here?

Sylvester (loudly): Just one!

Chanticleer: I gave up the crown when I got too old.

Homer: Do you still help govern with Sylvester and King Mortimer?

Chanticleer: No, I'm retired now; but in difficult matters, I still advise them.

Homer: Can you help me? Please tell them that I want to fly.

Chanticleer: I don't know. (Scratching his head while he thinks.) Your body isn't shaped like a Chicken's. You're different from us.

Homer: No, I'm not! We are part of the same family.

Just then Nigel and Priscilla pass by, and Sylvester chases after them.

Chanticleer: Jeremiah and Penelope have bodies shaped like the Doves. When they play with the Doves, they sometimes fly a bit.

Homer: Oh, can I play with Jeremiah and Penelope and tell them about my dreams?

Sylvester comes back, disappointed.

Sylvester (to Chanticleer): Your family is coming.

He goes back to the castle wall and lies down.

Chanticleer (pushing Homer away): Get away! I don't want my family to see us together.

Homer (sadly): But I need your help. (He looks at the sun.) Look how shiny it is.

Chanticleer: What is?

Homer: The sun.

The Chickens can be heard in the distance, coming closer.

Chanticleer: Get away from me!

He pushes Homer away and hides behind the tree. Homer climbs the tree and looks at the bright midday sun. Sylvester lies quietly as the Chickens enter.

Henrietta (looking up into the tree): His bed is empty. There's no one there. (She turns to Sylvester.) Sylvester, do you know where the Old King is?

Sylvester (pointing to Chanticleer behind the tree, he whispers): Behind the tree.

Henrietta (agitated): What? Is he hiding from me?

Chanticleer (preening himself as he appears from behind the tree): No, not hiding. Just attending to some of my duties.

Henrietta: You're the father of an important family. You should be taking care of us — not neglecting us.

Chanticleer: What are you accusing me of? How have I neglected you?

Henrietta: You didn't come to look after our welfare. The Geese went for a walk with the King and Queen, and we were left waiting for you. We'd still be there if I hadn't gotten up my courage and come looking for you.

She gives Jeremiah and Penelope a tender hug.

Chanticleer: Oh, I forgot. Please forgive me. It won't happen again. (He puts his wings around the two chicks.) Come, tomorrow we will be up before dawn, and we'll climb the highest hill in the area. We won't come back until sunset.

Homer appears from behind the tree trunk.

Homer (eagerly): Can I go with you?

Henrietta and her two chicks look at Homer in astonishment.

Henrietta: What's this? I don't believe what I'm seeing. (To Chanticleer.) Is this why you abandoned us today? For this ... (pointing at Homer) ... this ... creature?

Chanticleer: No, no. I can explain. I love my family.

Henrietta: Is this what kept you all morning?

Chanticleer: No! He's lost his way. He wants our help to get back home.

Homer: You'll help me then?

He rushes forward to grasp Chanticleer. Chanticleer pushes him away.

Henrietta (hugging Jeremiah and Penelope more closely to her): My sweet little things. See, your father has abandoned us. I feel sorry for you both.

Chanticleer: That's not true! I'm a good father! I love my family. I did not abandon them!

Chanticleer tries to hug his family, but Henrietta pushes him away. In the background are the sounds of Geese arriving. Sylvester hears them and quickly climbs on the tree.

Sylvester (loudly): Someone's coming!

Henrietta (to Chanticleer): I will report you to the King and Queen. They'll know what to do. Then we'll see how smart you are.

Sylvester (laughing): That's not the King and Queen. It's your nemesis.

Henrietta: Do you mean the Geese? Oh, my goodness, what'll we do now?

Homer (excitedly): The King is coming? (To Chanticleer.) Please tell him I need his help.

Chanticleer pushes Homer away. Henrietta gathers her two chicks to her side. Sylvester continues to make fun of them. Lucy Goose enters with her two goslings Bartholomew and Prunella in single file behind her. She looks around to see who is there. She spies Homer, and gasps.

Lucy: My lord! What's this? Is it real or some ghost sent to punish us for our misdeeds?

Homer approaches Lucy and her two goslings.

Henrietta (laughing derisively): Look at them. They all look alike. (She points at Homer, Lucy, and the goslings.) Surely our little stranger is a Goose.

Lucy (pushing Homer away from her): Don't you dare come any closer! Stay away from me and my precious little darlings. (She pulls Bartholomew and Prunella away. She looks again at Homer, then glances towards Henrietta.) Look at his feathers. He looks more like a Chicken than a Goose.

Henrietta (to Lucy): Look at the shape of your body and his. I'd say they were very similar. I'd say he was a Goose, all right!

Lucy (pushing Henrietta): His neck is crooked — just like the necks of your chicks.

Henrietta (pushing back): His legs and beak are exactly like those of your goslings.

> Both push each other several times, and soon they are scuffling.

Chanticleer (trying to intervene): Hey! Stop this nonsense! In Barnyardia, we're all friends. There is no need to insult one another. Stop it, I say!

> The sound of the Turkeys can be heard coming from the forest.

Sylvester (loudly so all can hear): Stop it! The King and Queen are coming!

Homer (excitedly): The King! The King is coming! He will help me!

> He turns in the direction of the approaching sounds.

Sylvester (with a worried look on his face, coming down out of the tree): Oh! What will happen now? I haven't got lunch prepared. (He turns angrily to Homer.) It's all your fault. You interrupted me while I was getting lunch ready. What will King Mortimer think of me?

Lucy (to Sylvester): Where's lunch? My darlings are hungry!

Henrietta: Yes! Where's lunch? My Sweeties are starving!

Chanticleer (to Sylvester): I will report this to the King. One of the rules in Barnyardia is that everyone performs his duties on time. We want our lunch on time.

Sylvester (apologetically): Don't think of me as lazy. I'm a good citizen, and a good chef, and I care about my duties. It's all his fault. (He points to Homer.) He made me late by taking up my time with his foolish dream of flying.

Chanticleer: We have to go to the kitchen to check on the food. Let's go.

> All turn and enter the castle, except Homer, who goes to the tree and starts to climb it.

Scene Two

Homer is sitting on the topmost branch of the tree, looking at the sun. From inside the castle come the sounds of food preparation. Sylvester appears, looking for Homer. He sees him in the tree.

Sylvester: You, there. Get down here this instant!

Homer (defiantly): No! I won't. I'm waiting for the King. He'll help me.

> King Mortimer and Queen Hortense can be heard in the distance, coming closer.

Sylvester: They're coming now. Get down from there quickly. (In a loud voice for all to hear.) The King and Queen are coming!

Homer (very excited now): I can see them! They're coming! I will tell the King that I want to fly. He'll help me. He can do anything he wants to.

> Sylvester climbs up the tree and brings Homer down with him.

Sylvester: I don't want the King to see you. Come down, and stay behind the tree. (He pushes Homer behind the tree.) Now stay there, and don't make a sound. And don't move a muscle — or else!

Homer (dejectedly): But I want to talk to the King. I want to tell him … (He sobs.)

Sylvester: Don't be silly! Stay here and be quiet! Stop crying!

> Sylvester turns to meet the King and Queen as they arrive. The Geese and the Chickens are first to enter, each family trying to out-strut the other. Sylvester arranges them in two

lines facing inward to form a lane through which the Royal Couple will pass. When they are in place, Sylvester gives the signal for the group to begin singing as King Mortimer and Queen Hortense enter.

All together (singing):
Welcome! Our Glorious Leader,
    welcome to your kingdom.
We are your faithful; we are your grateful.
    Welcome! Welcome!
The flowers are arranged; the red carpet's in place.
Welcome to your kingdom!
We are your guards; we are your servants.
Welcome! O Great One! Welcome!

King Mortimer (proudly, waving to all of them): Very good! Very good! Well done! Bravo! Bravo! Thank you, my loyal citizens, thank you. The Queen and I are very proud to see you all today. We are proud for all of you. We are thankful and grateful for such a splendid reception.

> King Mortimer and Queen Hortense seat themselves centrally. They are surrounded by the four little Chicks and Goslings, who seat themselves around the Royal Couple.

King Mortimer (patting the little ones as they try to snuggle closer): There, there, my sweet young things. You are the future of Barnyardia. (He calls.) Sylvester!

Sylvester: Yes, my lord.

King Mortimer: And what will you give us for our lunch today?

Sylvester (hesitantly): Whatever it is you want, my lord ... uh ... but ... uh ... before I set the table, my lord, I want to show you something new in Barnyardia.

King Mortimer: What! You haven't even set the table yet? What have you been doing? Don't you know it's almost past lunchtime!

Sylvester (quickly trying to cover his delay in getting lunch ready): What I mean is that before you begin to eat the delicious food I have prepared, I wish to inform you of a most unusual circumstance in Barnyardia today.

King Mortimer: What has happened? Has something gone wrong in Barnyardia?

Sylvester: Oh, no, my lord. Nothing's gone wrong. Everything is going just as you wish.

King Mortimer (reassured): Well, that's a relief. I was certain you could keep things running smoothly for me here in Barnyardia.

> Sylvester gets Homer from behind the tree and brings him to the Royal Couple.

Sylvester: My lord, take a look at this creature.

> They look at Homer with a surprised and quizzical look on their faces.

King Mortimer: And just exactly what is this? It's so puny. (He addresses Homer.) Who are you? Where have you come from, and what are you doing here in Barnyardia?

Homer (reverently and somewhat frightened in the King's presence): I'm just a little duckling. My name is Homer Duck, and my mother's name is Mathilda. I've lost my way, and I want help! Please, can you help me?

Sylvester (sarcastically): He says he wants to fly. And he says … — Pardon me, my lord, but these are his words … he says he's related to the White Storks. Can you believe it? (He laughs out loud, and the others also begin to laugh and sneer.)

Henrietta (to King Mortimer): I think he looks like a Goose!

Lucy (walking around Homer inspecting him): He has pale yellow feathers. I think he looks like a Chicken! A dead Chicken! (She laughs.) Look at his short wings. They're too stiff. How can he fly anywhere? (She turns to King Mortimer.) Maybe he can fly like the young Chickens do: from the top of the garbage can to the ground.

> Again she laughs and turns away.

King Mortimer (patting Penelope and Jeremiah): There, there. Don't mind what the Widow Goose says. She's just upset. You can fly quite high. (Turning to Bartholomew and Prunella, he pats them gently also.) And you, my dears, can also fly quite high. Here in Barnyardia we are all the same. There are no differences among us. We are all like teeth in a comb. All equal!

Homer (somewhat reassured by this display of kindness from the King): Excuse me. I'm looking for a way to get to the sun. Can you help me?

> All look at Homer in surprise. They had forgotten he was even there. There is a brief moment of silence as they readjust to his presence.

King Mortimer (the first to recover): What was that? What did he say?

Sylvester: He said he wants to touch the sun.

King Mortimer: But that's impossible!

Sylvester: I know, but that's what he said.

Homer (firmly): It is NOT impossible! If you help me, I will reach it!

King Mortimer: Do you know how far away the sun is from here?

Homer: Not exactly; I know it's a long way away, but not too far for me!

King Mortimer: The sun is a very long way from here! How can you ask for such an impossible thing?

Homer: It is **not** impossible. I just need you to point me in the right direction.

King Mortimer: Oh, I see. You want to know which direction to look to see the sun.

Homer: No, no. Not just to see the sun. I want to know which road to take to **find** the sun. When I know which way to go, I'll be able to fly high enough until I get close enough to **touch** the sun.

> They all burst out in laughter at such a preposterous statement.

King Mortimer (chuckling): You young people are all alike! You dream too much! (He turns to Sylvester.) Sylvester, don't pay any attention to this little one. He's just a dreamer, like these other youngsters.

> He points to the four Chicks and Goslings, who were beginning to believe Homer, but whose hopes were now dashed by the King's comments.

Henrietta (strutting around proudly): My little sweeties are different from those Ducks and Chickens. They're not like that at all.

> She pushes Lucy, who had gone to confront her.

Lucy (pushing Henrietta back): How dare you touch my feathers! Get away!

> They scuffle briefly again.

King Mortimer: My dears, stop this nonsense! You must show respect to each other. (He calls for Sylvester.) Sylvester! Come here! Stop them!

Sylvester: Yes, my lord. (He comes in.) I'm here. What can I do for you?

King Mortimer: Do something to stop this silly squabbling and fighting.

Sylvester: Yes, my lord. Your wish is my command.

> He goes to the scrapping couple and attempts to break them up. They continue a few moments.

King Mortimer: I'm so tired of all this. I just want to have lunch, and after lunch, I'll take a nap. Then maybe I'll go for a short walk. Ah! My work is never done.

> Sylvester has finally pried apart Lucy and Henrietta and pushes them away.

Sylvester: You two disappoint me. Is this any way to behave? You should have more respect in the presence of the King and Queen.

Henrietta (grabbing King Mortimer by the arm): King Mortimer, don't you agree that the Geese are the lowest class in Barnyardia?

Queen Hortense (who has been patient all this time): You can't touch the King like that! (She pushes Henrietta away.) Get back!

King Mortimer: I'm hungry. Sylvester, is lunch ready yet?

Sylvester (still trying to cover for his tardiness): But, my lord, what about the Duckling? Maybe you can get the squabbling families to agree to accept him in Barnyardia, while I put the finishing touches to lunch. OK?

> Homer climbs forlornly up the tree and sits looking at the sun. He sings:

Homer (singing):
Mother, dearest Mother! My sweet and darling Mother.
I miss your hugs at night, I need your warmth at night.
The road is long with many turns;
the time so short, it seems to burn.
Mother, Dearest Mother! My sweet and darling Mother.

You guide me on my road; you lead me to my dream.
Mother! I will be there! Mother! I will be near.
Mother, Dearest Mother! My sweet and darling Mother!

> Jeremiah, Penelope, Bartholomew, and Prunella all slowly climb the tree and sit with Homer. They sense a kinship with the little duckling. After all, the adults don't seem to understand their hopes and dreams, and they won't listen. Only Homer seems to understand their feelings; and they certainly understand his.

> Queen Hortense is moved by Homer's singing. She looks at him lovingly, and marvels at the reverence the other young ones have for him, as they, too, listen to the song. Finally she leans over and whispers to King Mortimer.

Queen Hortense (whispering gently): He's such a sweet thing. Don't you think that maybe we could adopt him as our own?

King Mortimer (also in a whisper): But he's so different from us.

Queen Hortense: Oh! Really? He has two wings, two feet, and a beak. So do we. Is that so different from us?

> In the tree, the five youngsters have huddled close together during the song, and from a distance they appear to be one single brood of birds. Sylvester, who has been watching and listening, notices this similarity and turns to King Mortimer.

Sylvester: My lord, look at them. They look like one family. They all look alike.

Henrietta (who has overheard Sylvester, is visibly upset): They are not alike at all! My little sweeties are taller and brighter. (She grabs Penelope and Jeremiah, and pulls them from their perch in a huff.) Come away from there!

Lucy (not to be outdone): **My** little darlings are unique. (She grabs Bartholomew and Prunella and pulls them down.) Don't associate with such riffraff!

Homer (pleading): Please don't take them away. We were only playing. Please!

> As Homer turns, he loses his balance and falls to the ground. Lucy helps him up.

Lucy: Don't be silly! Now stand up and behave! (She holds her beak.) Phew! You smell like a chicken. How disgusting!

Henrietta (offended, she turns to Chanticleer, who has been dozing): You cowardly old rooster. How can you just stand there and let that old Goose insult you like that?

Chanticleer (uncertain of himself or what he should say and to whom): I ... I ... can not ... will not ... allow anyone to insult me or any member of ... of my family. No one can offend my dignity. I am your retired King.

King Mortimer: My dear friends. My wonderful companions. The rules here in Barnyardia are very clear. We must all show respect for one another!

Sylvester (interrupting): My lord, you have yet to make a decision on the matter of our new guest. And your decision must come by sunset. I, for one, do not accept the behaviour of the Geese and the Chickens. It is not our custom or tradition to behave in this manner. Our rules do not permit anyone to be unkind to others.

King Mortimer: You are absolutely right! There is a simple solution. We will give our tiny friend here a new family name. One of the families of Barnyardia will adopt him, and he will become a citizen. Who will have him?

Queen Hortense (proudly): We will take care of him!

King Mortimer (not listening to the Queen): I say that the Geese shall adopt him.

Lucy (protesting as loudly as she can): No! No! Impossible! No way! No!

King Mortimer: But look at him. Look at his family background. He comes from the same roots as you do. You're almost related. (Angrily.) Besides, I'm hungry! Let's eat!

> There is a brief silence as they absorb the King's decree. Sylvester drags Homer behind the tree and whispers to him.

Sylvester: I told you not to make the King angry. Now stay here and be quiet, and don't get into any more trouble.

Homer (protesting): I want to fly! I want to fly to the sun!

Sylvester: For the last time now, stop that foolishness! You are in real danger. (Loudly for the rest to hear.) It's OK. He says he'll serve the King, and he does not need to be adopted by any family. (Whispering to Homer.) Now, promise to help me catch those pigeons tomorrow.

Homer: I will not!

Sylvester (quietly to Homer): You stubborn little fool. (He leads Homer out from behind the tree and addresses the King.) What is your pleasure regarding our friend here?

King Mortimer: So, it's settled then. If the Geese won't adopt him, then the Chickens shall. (To Homer.) Welcome to your new home. We are all very proud to have you as one of us.

Henrietta (protesting): No! It's unfair. We can't take a stranger in just like that!

Sylvester: And why not? It's perfectly reasonable. Besides, he'll serve the King, just like anybody else. (To himself.) I'd better go get lunch ready, or I'll be in big trouble!

He rushes off into the castle hurriedly.

Henrietta (not giving up easily): King Mortimer, my family and I have a right to protest against that which may bring discredit to our family, correct?

King Mortimer: Yes, that's true. What say you, friend Chanticleer?

Chanticleer (preening himself): Well, it's this way. I kind of feel sorry for the little tyke. (He gestures towards Homer.) And I think I … (He looks nervously towards Henrietta, who stands defiantly waiting for him to agree with her.) I think I agree with King Mortimer. And I ask my family to agree with me. Let's give him a chance to build his future with us here.

Henrietta (very angry): How can you do this to us? You demean all your family with such a statement. Just look at him! He's dirty, he comes from a home in muddy water in dirty ditches. I can't agree!

Homer (defiantly): Mother and I live in Lake Serenity, a big, clear lake. Its waters are the bluest of blue. And you can see the tiniest pebble on the bottom.

Henrietta (scoffing): That's the way it is with you Ducks and Geese. Because the water is dark, you say it is blue. You don't even know your colours.

Lucy (offended at this last remark): And you, my dear Henrietta. Have you forgotten your habit of digging around in garbage and filth, looking for worms?

They rush together and resume their scuffling again.

King Mortimer: Sylvester! Oh, Sylvester, come quickly! They're at it again!

Sylvester comes out and promptly breaks up the scuffle. When order is restored, he turns to the king.

Sylvester: And now, my lord, have you solved our little problem yet?

King Mortimer: No, not yet. I think we should first fill our stomachs. Things always seem to work better on a full stomach. Then we can solve our problem. Where's the food? I'm dying of hunger!

Sylvester: My lord, the table is set for your pleasure. Everyone is welcome to the feast.

The Geese and the Chickens gather their broods and strut into the castle, making sure not to look at each other.

Queen Hortense (smiling at Homer): What a cheerful soul. (To King Mortimer.) Let's take him with us.

King Mortimer: Remember your position in Barnyardia, Hortense. You are the Queen. (He takes her firmly by the arm and leads her into the castle.) Let's go to lunch.

They enter the castle, leaving Homer and Sylvester, who turns to Homer and winks.

Sylvester (to Homer): Now, my little friend, if you help me catch those pigeons, I'll help you with the King. Think about it while I fill my belly.

Sylvester follows the others into the castle. Homer stares at the sun for a short while, then begins pacing back and forth.

Homer: I wonder. Some day I'll be able to fly. I'm not giving up, regardless what the others say. I think I can do it. I believe I can. I **know** I can! (He sings):
I may be alone, and I may be small;
But my dream will grow some day.
I may be alone, and I may be small;
But my dream will come true some day.

> Jeremiah, Penelope, Bartholomew, and Prunella enter. They immediately surround Homer.

Homer (hugging his new friends): Some day … Some day we'll all fly to the sun! Somehow I've always imagined myself flying around the sun!

Henrietta enters, looking for her chicks. She sees them and rushes over.

Henrietta: What are you doing? Get away from him! He's dirty!

She pushes Homer away and hustles Jeremiah and Penelope back into the castle. Reluctantly, the little ones leave, casting a look back to Homer as they go. Homer and the goslings Bartholomew and Prunella hug together briefly as they look towards the sun. Lucy enters, and also looks around for her goslings. She spies them, rushes over, and quickly takes them under her wing.

Lucy: Come, my little darlings. King Mortimer is about to give some advice to his subjects. I want you to listen to him.

Homer: Please let them stay a while longer. Please don't take them away.

Lucy (pushing Homer away): Get away, you foolish little duckling!

> She takes her two offspring and they turn to leave. Prunella gives a little wave to Homer as she is ushered into the castle by her mother.

Homer (continues to sing):
I may be alone, and I may be tiny;
But I'm growing stronger day by day.
I may be alone, and I may be tiny;
But my dream will come true some day.

> Homer leans on the tree trunk and falls asleep. The haunting refrain lingers in the air.

ACT TWO
Scene One

Kingdom of Barnyardia; dusk has fallen. The sun has almost set. Homer is standing forlornly by himself, absentmindedly gazing into space. Chanticleer enters. He looks around and sees that they are alone. He comes over quickly and quietly to Homer.

Chanticleer (in a quiet, conspiratorial voice): Come with me. I'll help you. I can show you how to fly!

Homer: Really? Can you really show me how to fly to the sun?

Chanticleer: Well, I'll show you how to fly. The sun is too far away to fly to it.

Homer (looking at the setting sun): Look, it's almost gone.

Chanticleer: You'll have to climb to the top of the tree to see it better. You'll also be safe there. Come.

Homer: I'll have to do a lot of preparation if I'm going to fly to the sun.

Chanticleer: Right now, you'd be better off if you climbed a tree. I heard the King say that you had to be punished. Come, it will be dark soon.

Homer: I'll wait here until morning so I can see the sun rising.

Chanticleer: It'd be better for you to watch the moon. It'll be coming up over those hills.

Homer: But the sun is bigger and brighter than the moon. I want to see it. I'll wait here.

Chanticleer: You're certainly a stubborn little bird.

> He takes Homer by the hand, and they both climb the tree. The sun sets slowly. It is dark. After a few moments, a figure appears furtively from around a corner of the castle. It is Sylvester wearing a mask. He is looking for Homer. He climbs the tree.

Sylvester (to Homer): Are you a friend of this old rooster Chanticleer?

Homer (frightened): Who ... who are ... you?

Sylvester: Never mind who I am. Come with me and be quiet!

> He takes Homer with him. On the way down, his mask slips and Homer sees who it is.

Homer: Oh, it's you, Sylvester. I'm scared.

Sylvester: Right, it's me. I'll help save your life, but don't forget tomorrow you have to help me. I want to catch just one of those pigeons! King Mortimer has decided to take tough action against you. I'll hide you in the kitchen. You'll be safe there, and you can also find something to eat.

Homer: I don't want your food! And I won't help you catch the pigeons!

Sylvester: You're a stubborn duckling.

> He drags Homer away with him. Chanticleer looks at them briefly, but sleep soon overcomes him.

Scene Two

It is night. The moon is rising above the hills. The trees and hills are silhouetted against the sky. Occasionally, night insects can be heard, perhaps an occasional frog or cricket. Henrietta, Penelope, and Jeremiah enter from the right; Lucy, Prunella, and Bartholomew enter from the left; Sylvester, King Mortimer, and Queen Hortense enter from the castle. They are dressed in black and white, and are looking for Homer.

King Mortimer (in a half-whisper): Do you see him? Is he here?

Queen Hortense: Perhaps he's in the tree.

King Mortimer: I'll call Sylvester. He'll find him for us. (Calling quietly.) Sylvester! Where are you? I need you. Come here at once!

Queen Hortense: Maybe he's busy working on a new recipe.

King Mortimer (calling more loudly): SYLVESTER! WHERE ARE YOU! COME HERE!

Sylvester enters running and out of breath.

Sylvester (panting): Yes … my lord. … Here I am!

King Mortimer: Have you seen the young Duck? Do you know where he is?

Sylvester: No, my lord, I don't. I've been working on tomorrow's menu.

King Mortimer: I must have a solution to this problem. I want you to find him. Now!

Sylvester (suddenly remembering): Oh, now I remember. I saw him earlier talking to Chanticleer. Maybe he showed the young Duck how to get out of Barnyardia and he left before sunset.

Henrietta (astonished): Are you saying that Chanticleer let the Duck escape?

Sylvester: I didn't say he did. I only said maybe he did.

King Mortimer: Well if he showed the Duck how to get away from us, he's a traitor. (Looking around.) Where is he? Has anyone seen Chanticleer?

Sylvester climbs the tree to where Chanticleer is sleeping.

Sylvester: Here he is, my lord. Sound asleep.

He pushes Chanticleer, who falls to the ground and staggers to his feet, unsure of what happened to him. Immediately he is surrounded by the others.

Henrietta: Did you do what Sylvester says? Huh? Did you? You good-for-nothing!

Chanticleer (still dazed): Huh? What are you saying? Did I do what?

Henrietta: You've done a horrible thing. You've betrayed us all!

Chanticleer: What are you talking about? Who is betrayed? I'm your retired King! I don't know anything about any betrayal. What's going on here?

King Mortimer: You are a traitor! You forgot your duties and obligations to Barnyardia. You must be punished. (To Sylvester.) Take him away and tie him up. We will punish him later, according to the laws of Barnyardia.

Sylvester quickly ties Chanticleer up.

Chanticleer (protesting): What have I done? How can you do this to me? I'm a king!

King Mortimer: You may be a king, but the law applies to everyone equally. We must all be faithful and patriotic to our country or suffer the consequences. It is only in this way that our country can stay strong. We must all be honest, true, and faithful to Barnyardia. Long live Barnyardia! (To Sylvester.) Put him behind bars!

> Sylvester carries Chanticleer off and exits. The others follow after him in a march.
>
> Homer enters slowly, deep in thought. He comes to the tree and slowly climbs it.

Homer: What will happen to the rooster **now**? He really wanted to help me.

> Sylvester enters looking for Homer. He sees him in the tree and climbs up to him.

Sylvester: Why did you leave so soon? You were safely hidden. Nobody would have found you. Come with me before they come back and find you here. Besides, I need your help tomorrow morning.

Homer: I told you I wouldn't help you catch the pigeons. They're my friends.

Sylvester: Look! All I want to do is help save your life. Can't you understand that? (A noise is heard.) Shh! Do you hear that? They're coming back. (He drags Homer behind the tree.) Now you stay here, and be quiet!

> King Mortimer and Queen Hortense enter.

King Mortimer: Sylvester. Come here!

Sylvester: Yes, my lord.

King Mortimer: Have you seen the duckling recently?

Sylvester (very nervous): No, my lord. No. ... Uh ... I said he left. Or

... uh ... rather, I think he left. Excuse me, but I've got to make sure that Chanticleer isn't loose. It's time to set a punishment for him, don't you think? Perhaps we should go.

King Mortimer: Perhaps you're right. Let's go. (He takes Sylvester aside.) You go ahead and get things ready. When you're done, call us. (Sylvester exits.)

> Homer appears from behind the tree, and Queen Hortense sees him.

Queen Hortense (surprised): Oh, look who's here! He hasn't left after all. (She approaches Homer.) You are the clever one, aren't you? (To King Mortimer.) I want to take care of this dear little soul. May I, please!

King Mortimer: But what will the rest of them say? And what about the Geese, and especially the Chickens; what will they think of us?

Queen Hortense: Well, we'll just ... we'll just have to take our chances. This duckling is very much like their own babies. He has characteristics of both the Geese and the Chickens.

King Mortimer: You know that both families refused to accept him. Neither of them wants him to become part of Barnyardia. I have to respect their feelings.

Queen Hortense (indignantly): And what about my feelings? Don't you have to respect my feelings, too? (She hugs Homer.) When I first laid eyes on him, I felt like a mother to him. Please, Mortimer, convince the Geese and the Chickens to accept Homer as part of Barnyardia. I ... that is ... we will take care of him as though he were our very own.

King Mortimer: I can't do that. I can't take the chance of losing my crown over this scrawny little creature! You ask too much.

Queen Hortense: Please, Mortimer, I beg you. Do it for me … for us.

King Mortimer: But if they don't agree, we could lose everything. I might no longer be King; you might no longer be Queen. That's a lot to risk.

Queen Hortense: Maybe so, but I would gladly give it all up for him.

King Mortimer: Would you like to see Henrietta as Queen of Barnyardia?

Queen Hortense: I don't care who becomes Queen.

King Mortimer (defiantly): Well, I care about this crown. I will not give it up to anyone! (He points to Homer.) I want this scrawny bundle of feathers to be punished according to our laws. I am King. I have spoken!

Queen Hortense (sadly): My poor dear Mortimer. You are already quite old. Have you given any thought to who might inherit your crown someday?

> Mortimer is momentarily shocked as he realizes his mortality. He looks at Homer. Sylvester enters as the king continues to gaze at Homer.

Sylvester (calling): My lord! My lord! (He spies Homer, and stops in his tracks.) So, I see he's back. So he didn't leave after all. (To King Mortimer.) My lord, everything is in readiness. Chanticleer is tied up securely. Everyone is gathered and waiting to see his punishment before they go to bed.

King Mortimer (despondently): Very well. Traitors first; strangers next.

> He takes Hortense by the arm and they exit.

Sylvester (to Homer): Do you fully understand the meaning of the

King's words? You are doomed! But I might still be able to help you; if you help me. Understand?

He exits after the king. Thoroughly depressed, Homer slowly climbs back up the tree and gazes blankly at the moon. It is midnight. The moon shines brightly, and the stars twinkle in the clear sky. As Homer sits gazing, he addresses the moon.

Homer: Dear Moon, how beautiful you look tonight. O Sweet Gentle Moon, can you help me? Please, I need a hug tonight. Take me into your gentle arms and hold me as my mother used to. I miss her very much. Dear Moon, I do so want to fly! I want to fly around the sun! Tomorrow is a new day, and maybe a new life. The sun will rise; every living creature will try to achieve his or her own dream. Dear Moon, tell the sun that I will wait here until tomorrow, when I, too, will begin searching for my dream to come true. I will never give up. (He climbs down from his perch.) O Sweet Gentle Moon, how friendly your face is.

(He sings.)
My faithful friends, do not disturb my dreams.
My dear companions, do not break my wish.
I was born from Momma's dream.
My wishes call me; my dreams await me.
Whether they be roses or thorns,
My dreams will all come true.

As Homer sings, Penelope, Jeremiah, Bartholomew, and Prunella enter. They were attracted by the singing. They stand for a while, watching and listening to Homer from a distance. As the song ends, they come closer. Homer sees them and beckons them to come closer.

Come, my friends. It is such a nice night. It is warm, calm, and bright. Come. Join me and we will sing, and dance, and play together.

The five youngsters form a circle and dance and sing and play together for a few minutes. Finally, they slow down and fall to the ground exhausted. Jeremiah is first to break the silence. He addresses Homer.

Jeremiah: Why do you want to fly? Stay here with us. We'll have a lot of fun together.

Homer: Well, I've always had a dream of flying some day. I want my dream to come true. Everyone has a dream. Mine is to fly! I want to touch the sun!

Penelope: Mother says the sun is far, far away, and very hot. We can't touch it. We'll scorch ourselves!

Homer: Sometimes we have to work very hard to make our dreams come true.

Jeremiah: But, how can you fly so far? You don't have very strong wings.

Bartholomew: Maybe we can all fly together! I'll bet then we'll be strong enough.

Prunella (very excited): Yes, yes! Let's try it. Let's try right now!

Homer (calmly): No, tomorrow is soon enough. After the sun comes up.

Bartholomew (eagerly): Can we fly with you, too? Please!

Homer: No, I'm afraid not. Your mothers need you here. I'll have to fly alone.

Bartholomew (dejected): And what about **your** mother? Doesn't she need **you**?

Homer (sadly): Yes, she does. She's home waiting for me.

Prunella: Then why don't you go back to her?

Homer (proudly): Because first, I have to achieve my dream. I have to find the way to the sun. Then I'll fly, and after that I'll go home!

> Henrietta and Lucy enter, looking for their young ones. Homer and the four young birds cling to each other almost desperately as their mothers approach. The four begin shouting and crying aloud that they want to fly.

All (separately and creating quite a clamor): We want to fly! We want to fly to the sun! We want to be with Homer. Please let us fly! We want to fly!

Lucy (quickly gathering Bartholomew and Prunella to her side, and pushing them to a far corner, away from Homer and the others): What an embarrassment you are to us! How can you be seen in such company? Don't you know any better? Haven't I taught you to behave properly? Shame on you!

Henrietta (not to be outdone): The only shame and embarrassment is that Chickens were in the presence of Ducks and **Geese**!

> She grabs Jeremiah and Penelope by their necks and drags them away. As Lucy and Henrietta drag their young ones away, Homer slinks behind the tree and sits down, very sad and dejected. He settles himself down, curls his head beneath his wing, and goes to sleep.

Scene Three

It is early morning. The sun has not yet risen; a faint glow can be seen in the eastern sky. There is a promise of a bright, clear day. Homer is sleeping on the ground beside the tree. Suddenly, loud, frightened voices are heard inside the castle. Sylvester comes running out.

Sylvester (calling aloud): Homer! Homer! Where are you? (He sees Homer and rushes over to him. He shakes him by the shoulder.) Wake up, Homer! Wake up!

Homer (waking up, frightened by the noise): What's the matter? Who are you?

Sylvester: Boy, are you in for it now! You're really going to get it! What have you been telling the young Chickens and Geese? They say they want to fly! You'd better come with me. Get away from here while you still can.

Homer: No! I'm staying here. I'm waiting for the sun to rise.

> Angry voices can be heard inside. They are getting louder and closer.

Sylvester: Do you hear that?

Homer: What is it? What do you want me to do?

Sylvester: Come with me!

Homer (reluctantly): But look at the sky. The sun will rise soon. I can see the first rays.

Sylvester: Will you forget the sun! Come, hide yourself. Quickly now!

He drags Homer behind the tree to safety before the others arrive.

Homer (still protesting): I don't want to hide! I've done nothing wrong!

King Mortimer, Queen Hortense, the Chickens, and the Geese enter, looking for Homer.

King Mortimer (angrily): He has disrupted our peaceful way of life with his silly talk of flying. He must be punished as an enemy of the people! Where is he?

Homer (very frightened, he whispers to Sylvester): Please, save me! Don't let them get me. I'll do anything you ask! Just keep me from harm.

Sylvester: Then give up your silly dream about wanting to fly!

Homer: But I can't. I just can't. I **want** to fly!

Meanwhile, the others have been searching for Homer and have not been successful. They decide to leave. All go back inside, making grumbling noises.

Sylvester: You have no choice. If you want to live, give up your silly notion of flying!

Homer: Will you promise to protect me until the sun rises?

Sylvester: No way! (He hesitates for a moment.) Well, wait a minute. Maybe there is a way. Didn't you just say you'd do anything for me if I saved you?

Homer: Yes.

Sylvester: Well, first you have to forget about flying and swear to help me; then I'll protect you with my sharp claws. Nobody would dare harm you. You could live here forever like a prince with me as your protector. What do you say?

Homer: No! I'll never agree to that! I'll fight by myself if I have to. I will not give up my dream for you, or anyone else! I don't need your help!

Sylvester (nonchalantly): Very well, then. Have it your way, but you will get into a lot of trouble if you keep talking about flying! (He takes a few steps, pauses, and turns back to face Homer.) Now listen to me carefully, my little friend. Since you refused to help me, I can't help you. I'm leaving. Good-bye! And Good Luck!

Homer: Where are you going?

Sylvester: Oh, nowhere in particular. I just thought I might go tell everyone that you went home to your beautiful Lake Serenity.

He saunters slowly back into the castle.

Homer (almost to himself): But I'm not going back. At least not yet, anyway. I'm going to pursue my dream. I'm going to fly!

There is a sudden commotion inside. Angry voices are heard coming from the castle.

Homer (timidly to himself, reassuringly): I'm not scared of them. Not anymore.

The searchers enter, see Homer, and surround him.

King Mortimer: There he is! We've found him. You can't get away now. We've got you, you troublemaker. You won't get away this time!

Homer (facing them defiantly): I'm not afraid of you! I've done nothing wrong! I can fight all of you!

King Mortimer: Quick, grab him before he gets away! Lock him up where he won't be able to see the sun rise. Maybe that will stop his foolish dream!

Homer (pleading): Please, King Mortimer. Let me go. Don't destroy my dreams!

King Mortimer: And why not, pray tell? You came here uninvited; proceeded to put foolish ideas into our children's heads; almost caused a riot; got fights started among our people. You're nothing but bad luck for us! Grab him!

> They surge forward as if to attack Homer. He quickly jumps up and grabs the lowest tree branch, and pulls himself up out of their immediate reach. Hortense, during all this, has been trying unsuccessfully to prevent them from grabbing Homer. She has finally had enough, and defiantly stands in front of the tree with her back to it, protecting Homer from their further attacks.

Queen Hortense (fiercely): Stop this! Get back! All of you! I will not allow anyone to harm a single feather on his back! Do you hear me?

> They all freeze in their tracks. They look towards King Mortimer.

King Mortimer (loudly, but firmly): Stand back! I'll handle this. I am the King! My orders have to be obeyed. (He comes close to Hortense and whispers in her ear.) Dear Hortense, listen to me. Our responsibility is to protect Barnyardia from intruders, and especially from those who would destroy our way of life. This Duck (pointing to Homer) has caused a great deal of trouble for us already. Isn't that enough? He must be punished. Don't you see? (He turns to the crowd.) Where's Sylvester? Get Sylvester here! He'll get the rascal down.

> Sylvester enters.

Sylvester: I'm here, my lord. Ready to do your bidding. What do you need?

King Mortimer (pointing to Homer): Get that rascal down here.

Sylvester (pushing his way to the tree): Stand back! Let me handle this!

I'll take care of that good-for-nothing troublemaker.

He climbs the tree.

Queen Hortense (with a note of warning to Sylvester): You be careful, now. If **you** harm him, you will be in big trouble yourself! Bring him down safely!

> As Sylvester pursues Homer, Homer jumps from branch to branch. Sylvester chases him but can't seem to corner him. He calls to the crowd below.

Sylvester: Friends, form a circle around the base of the tree to catch him if he should jump down. That way he won't be able to escape.

They form a circle just as Homer prepares to jump to the ground.

Queen Hortense: Don't jump, Homer. It's too high. You'll hurt yourself!

> Homer jumps. The others converge on him. In the scuffle, Jeremiah and Bartholomew, who are trying to protect Homer from the others, bump into each other and fall down. They seem to be slightly dazed. Henrietta and Lucy, seeing their young ones fall down, immediately rush to their aid.

Henrietta (soothingly to Jeremiah): There, there, my sweetie. Are you hurt? Oh, you've lost some of your feathers! Are you OK? Where does it hurt?

Lucy (making cooing sounds over Bartholomew): My darling, tell Momma where it hurts. Can you get up? Oh, look! You're bleeding! Help!

Henrietta: This is all that fool Duck's fault. Where is he? I'll strangle him!

> Homer has taken refuge behind the tree. Henrietta and

Lucy see him there and run to get him. They are stopped by Hortense.

Queen Hortense: Get back! Get away from him! Don't you touch one single feather on him! (She turns to Mortimer.) Isn't he a proud fighter? He may be tiny, but he's tough! (To Homer.) I'm so proud of you! (To Mortimer.) Won't you help him? Please! For my sake!

King Mortimer: I … I … don't know. It's not only my decision to make.

Meanwhile, Jeremiah and Bartholomew have recovered and come forward.

Jeremiah: Where's Homer? Is he all right?

Bartholomew: Yes, where is our little friend? Homer, are you OK?

Henrietta: He's OK for now. But he'll be punished for what he's done to you.

Jeremiah: No! Don't punish him. We're not hurt. He's our friend. We want to fly with him at sunrise.

Henrietta: King Mortimer, did you hear that? Did you hear what Jeremiah just said?

Bartholomew: I want to fly, too! I want to fly with Homer!

Lucy: King Mortimer, you must do something! If they all fly away, there will be nobody left. Barnyardia will become a ghost yard. Barnyardia will be empty!

The sun rises and casts its bright rays across the land. Homer sees it and jumps with glee. He scrambles quickly up the tree to enjoy the sunshine. He sits transfixed, with his face towards the east.

Homer (very excited): Oh, look! Isn't it beautiful? So warm and gentle!

I want to touch it. (He sings):
The sky removes its nighttime mantle.
How beautiful is the morning sun!
Its golden rays are warm and gentle.
How wonderful is the morning sun!

> As Homer sings, the four youngsters are entranced. Soon they come out of their reverie and gather around King Mortimer, jumping and shouting, clamoring that they want to fly.

All four youngsters: We want to fly! We want to fly! The sun is rising! Let us go with Homer. We want to fly to the sun and touch it, too!

Sylvester (to the King): Well, my lord. It appears that the solution to your problem is not an easy one. It's pretty hard to ignore the clamoring of all the young ones. After all, they are the future of Barnyardia. You'll have to consider their wishes, too. This younger generation is pretty adamant. They know what they want. You'll have to make up your mind. In order to save Barnyardia, it looks like you'll have to help Homer get his wish.

King Mortimer: You may be right, Sylvester. (He addresses the assembled throng.) What do you say? Do you all agree? Do we help Homer achieve his dream?

Henrietta: No! I do not agree!

Sylvester: But Henrietta, we have to abide by the King's decision, whatever it is.

Lucy: It's just unfair. We're also part of Barnyardia. We have a right to take part in the decision-making. We cannot agree to something that will put us all in danger!

Hortense: Look, I'll be responsible for Homer. By myself, if necessary!

Sylvester: I agree with King Mortimer! I think we should help Homer make his dream come true.

> Jeremiah, Bartholomew, Prunella, and Penelope join hands in a circle around King Mortimer and begin dancing and singing.

All four (in unison): We're all going to fly! We're all going to fly! We'll fly to the sun with Homer! Hip! Hip! Hooray!

King Mortimer: Wait a minute! Hold on a second. It's too early for you to fly. First you have to learn how to fly; then you have to have strong wings.

Jeremiah: We've learned lots of things from Homer already.

King Mortimer: But not how to fly!

Bartholomew: Look! The sun is close to the hills. We have to fly soon or it'll be too late.

Lucy (to the King): My good King Mortimer, please do something! You have to stop this wild dream of theirs!

Bartholomew: If you try to stop us, we'll run away! And you'll never get us back.

King Mortimer (calling, almost desperately): Sylvester! Sylvester, where are you?

Sylvester: Right here, my lord.

> He stands beside Homer but doesn't move.

King Mortimer: Sylvester, I need your help and advice. This is too big a decision for me to make alone. What do you think?

Sylvester (bending down to whisper to Homer): See, I told you I was his right hand? And even if **you've** decided not to help me, **I've**

decided to help **you**. (He straightens up and walks proudly towards King Mortimer.) I think that poor little Homer here needs your help. I suggest ... that you use your ... miraculous magic powers ... to help him get his wish. ... (Pleading.) ... Please, my revered and honoured King, grant this humble, honest little servant his wish. Perform a miracle from your boundless basket of miracles and enable him to fly to the sun!

King Mortimer: Very well, then, my esteemed and learned friend. It shall be done!

> They march triumphantly back into the castle. Even Lucy and Henrietta have relented and accepted King Mortimer's decision, albeit somewhat reluctantly. Only Homer remains. He sits smiling and looking at the sun. He sings softly to himself.

Homer (singing):
I may be alone, and I may be tiny,
But I'm growing stronger day by day...
I may be alone, and I may be tiny,
But my dream will come true some day.

> Suddenly he faints and falls unconscious to the floor.

> King Mortimer and Queen Hortense enter, followed by the others. They surround Homer. They are dressed in white gowns and wearing white skull caps. Homer stirs, wakes up, then sits up. He looks around in amazement.

Homer: Mother, is that you? Mother! Where are you? I need you!

> He tries to get up but is unable to. He falls back again. King Mortimer starts to puff up his feathers. A strong wind begins to blow. It gets stronger. There is distant thunder and lightning. It gets closer and louder. The trees

begin to shake and creak. It gets progressively worse. It seems that everything in Barnyardia is trembling. Mortimer's eyes are closed, and he seems to be deep in concentration. He speaks slowly, reverently almost as if he were praying.

King Mortimer: O Almighty Spirit ... Creator of the Universe ... hear my most fervent prayer. ... I beseech you, have the gentleness and kindness to grant this harmless, innocent child his one and only dream.

Homer (stirring): Mother! Is that you? I'm frightened, Mother. Where are you? ... Momma!

King Mortimer: Almighty and Omnipotent Being ... I implore you. Send this tiny little one the strength to reach his goal. He asks so little, yet deserves so much.

> Homer slowly floats up from the ground. He floats effortlessly in the air and is rising ever so slowly. He flaps his wings, as if testing them.

Homer (flapping his wings in disbelief): Mother, look, I'm flying! I'm flying, Mother!

> King Mortimer and Queen Hortense move closer together. They follow Homer, who slowly continues to rise.

Queen Hortense (tearfully): We've lost him, Mortimer. We've lost him!

> Homer flies yet higher. He is almost out of sight. They all wave their handkerchiefs gently to him as he disappears into the dark sky.

King Mortimer: Good-bye, Homer. Enjoy your dream, because to dream is to live, and to live is to achieve your dreams.

Only the distant echo of Homer's voice can be heard, fading away into the distance.

Homer: I'm flying! I'm flying to the sun! I knew I could! Mother, look! I'm flying! **I can fly!**

End of Part One

Part Two

Against the Odds

In Part II, Homer battles Against the Odds as he faces Mother Nature and all her powers as they try to stop him from going farther on his mission to fly to the sun.

Homer took the first step in Part I by having a dream to guide his actions. He is now able to fly. His next step will not be an easy one, because Nature will now challenge him. Part II pits the elements of nature: Wind, Tornado, and Dark Cloud against Homer. Which of these will emerge victorious?

Read Part II – "Against the Odds" for the answer!

The dream grows...

In Part I, "A Duckling's Dream," we met Homer, an ambitious and determined duckling. His one dream was to fly to the sun. He met and overcame many obstacles on his quest. With the support of his young friends and the supernatural powers of the king of Barnyardia, Homer eventually realized the beginning of his dream — he could fly! As Part I ended, Homer was on his way, flying to the sun.

In Part II, "Against the Odds," you will read how our intrepid Homer challenges the very elements of Nature, and how he copes with a vicious storm thrown in his path.

The Characters

Homer   a duckling

Mathilda   a duck, Homer's mother

Nigel   a male pigeon

Priscilla   a female pigeon

King Mortimer   a turkey tom, king of Barnyardia

Wind   an invisible element of nature;
                          only its voice and sound are heard

Dark Cloud   a changing element of nature,
                          changing shape as Wind blows

Tornado   another powerful element of nature,
                          made of swirling dust and debris

Rainbow   colourful lights emanating from below,
                          bathing the sky in never-ending
                          colours

The Setting

A stormy day, somewhere in the heavens high above the earth.

Prologue

It is peaceful in the Kingdom of Barnyardia. The golden sun seems suspended between the sky and the earth as it travels slowly to the west. King Mortimer is outside his castle in the yard, sitting with his back against a tree trunk. He is by himself, looking thoughtfully at the sun.

King Mortimer (musing to himself): Did I do the right thing? Or was I just feeling sorry for the little tyke? (He looks at the sun.) He was only dreaming. Every child wants to touch the sun. (He gets up and walks a few steps.) I'm worried about him! I didn't want him to fly, but he's done it. (He sits and looks at the sky.) Where is he now? Maybe he has crashed somewhere in the forest? He's not strong enough to fly against Wind. If the weather gets bad, his life will be in danger. He is so small. He will be frightened of the lightning and thunder! (He looks toward the west.) I knew it! This is the storm season. Big black clouds are coming toward us. (He calls, knowing that he cannot be heard.) Homer! Homer ... come back. A big storm is brewing! Come back! You can't fly now. (He sits nervously.) I made a bad decision by asking for help to give him the power to fly.

> Just then Mathilda Duck's voice is heard calling from within the nearby forest.

Mathilda: Homer! Homer! My son! Where are you?

> King Mortimer, hearing the voice, gets up and looks at the sky, searching for Homer.

King Mortimer (terrified): What have I done? What can I tell his mother? Oh, Almighty Spirit, bring him back safely to his mother.

Mathilda appears. She is searching for Homer in every nook and cranny.

Mathilda (sobbing): Homer! Where are you? I need you. I don't want to lose you.

King Mortimer approaches Mathilda politely.

King Mortimer: Why are you crying, my dear?

Mathilda (crying): I've lost my son. I'm looking for my little Homer.

King Mortimer (pretending that nothing is wrong): Don't worry. I'm sure he's around here somewhere.

Mathilda: But I've looked everywhere for him. I looked all around the lake, and I asked everyone I saw, but nobody has seen my little one.

She cries more loudly than before.

King Mortimer (hugs her): Don't worry. Calm down, my dear. The young people these days are always curious to discover new things. He's probably doing some exploring somewhere. (He looks up at the sky.) I'm sure he's safe wherever he is.

Mathilda (sees Mortimer's gaze heavenward): Do you mean he's up there in the trees?

King Mortimer (hesitantly): No … he's higher than the trees.

Mathilda (somewhat bewildered): Higher than this tree? (She points to the tallest tree.)

King Mortimer: Yes, I believe so. It seems he wanted to try flying a little bit.

Mathilda: Do you know where he is now? I want to see him.

King Mortimer: I don't know where he is at this moment, but I'm sure he'll be back soon.

Mathilda: But I'd like to see him now. He's the only son I have.

> At that moment a big, dark cloud covers the sky, completely hiding the sun. Everything becomes black. It is dark. Lightning strikes several nearby trees. Thunder is heard beyond the hills. Wind starts to blow.

King Mortimer (terrified): O! Almighty Creator of the Universe! Hear my prayer. I beseech you … have the gentleness and kindness to protect little Homer from dangerous thunderstorms and bring him back to his dear mother unharmed.

Mathilda (terrified): Do you know where my son is?

King Mortimer: He's flying somewhere between the earth and the sky.

> They both look up at the sky.

Mathilda (excited): My little one, flying? Really? All on his own?

King Mortimer: Yes, he's flying. He's full of energy. He struggled so hard to get what he wanted.

Mathilda (more excited): Do you mean to say that my son is flying above those trees?

King Mortimer: Even higher.

> Mathilda tries to climb onto the tree but Wind blows her away.

Mathilda: I want to see my son. (She falls to the ground.) Where is my little one? Wind is so strong, it's impossible to fly against it. (She calls desperately.) Homer! My little Homer! Where are you? Please come back!

> King Mortimer helps her get up.

King Mortimer: My dear Mathilda! Don't worry about him. He'll make it back. He's just trying to show us how strong and brave he is. He wants to show us what he can do when he grows up. No harm will come to him. He's not far from us.

Mathilda: He's so little. Wind will blow him away, and I'll never see him again.

King Mortimer: I helped him … because he is a capable and determined child, he could make the impossible become possible. Don't worry. We will see him soon.

> Both look at the sky fearfully. A dark cloud covers the sky. Lightning strikes the earth. Thunder crashes all around them. Wind blows strongly, moving trees and shattering their branches. Everything in the kingdom is being twisted into a mass of vegetation. The rain falls slowly at first, then swiftly it becomes a heavy downpour, like a waterfall, cascading from a high cliff. King Mortimer and Mathilda are terrified and run into the castle for shelter. Everything becomes dark. All that remains is the sound of nature mixed with the sound of frightened voices.

ACT ONE
Scene One

It is past midday, the sky is clear and blue, and the sun is traveling on its destined journey to the west. Several big, dark clouds appear on the horizon. A gentle breeze is blowing, birds fly randomly, enjoying their freedom. A large, black cloud begins to move rapidly toward the middle of the sky, partially obscuring the rays of the sun. Into this scene comes Homer, flying and singing joyfully.

Homer (singing):

> Yesterday I was crawling; ... today I am jumping.
> Yesterday I was dreaming; ... today I am flying.
> Tomorrow is my future. ... For the sun I am aiming!
> Tomorrow I'll be near. ... My future will be clear!

> Suddenly Dark Cloud covers the sky. Wind blows. Lightning flashes. Thunder echoes all around. Homer struggles against Wind as he tries to fly higher.

Homer (bewildered): Who is pushing me down?

> He covers his eyes with his tiny wings as he is blown by Wind into Dark Cloud.

Homer: Where is the sun? (He struggles against Wind.) Don't push me. Who are you?

> Wind laughs loudly. The echo of its laughter seems to come from all directions.

Wind (in a haunting voice): I am Wind! ...The All-powerful Wind! ... The Howling Wind!

Homer (struggling against the blowing wind): Where are you?

Wind (laughing): You can't see me, little one, but I'm all around you!

Homer: Why not?

Wind: Because I'm invisible. Nobody can see me, but everyone can see what I have done and how strong and powerful I am.

Homer: How can you speak to me if I can't see you?

Homer flies around, looking for Wind.

Wind (laughing): You can't touch me! I'm everywhere. You can only feel my strength.

Homer: Why are you pushing me away?

Wind: I'm only doing my job. I've no personal feelings towards any creature on earth.

Wind blows even more strongly, blowing Homer away.

Homer (screaming): Stop it! What are you doing? Why are you pushing me away? Where are you? Show yourself. What are you afraid of, you coward?

He struggles to fly up, but he hardly moves his tiny wings.

Wind (laughing loudly): O! My little one! You are but dust flying in the air. I can blow you anywhere I wish.

Homer (struggling): I am not dust. I'm someone struggling to make a place in this world.

Wind: Are you challenging me? Listen, little one! Nothing can stand up to me. I'm the strongest element in the universe. I am known as the Undefeatable Wind. (The laughing gets louder.) But sometimes I can be gentle, too.

Homer (still struggling against Wind): Then please stop pushing so hard, and be gentle now!

Wind (blowing even more strongly): I'll show you my gentleness after I've shown you my power!

Homer: You have blown me off course. Let me fly on my journey to the sun.

Wind: I can't do that. I have a job to do. Besides, I'm blowing the clouds so they can do their job, too.

> Dark Cloud covers the sky completely. It becomes very dark. Wind continues blowing. Homer disappears into Dark Cloud. Only his voice is heard.

Homer: I can't see anything. Where is the blue sky? Where is the sun?

> Dark Cloud changes shape as Wind blows it across the sky. Finally Dark Cloud speaks.

Dark Cloud: Of course you can't see the blue sky and the sun anymore.

Homer: Get out of my way.

Dark Cloud: This is my job. By the way, I'm full of water. You have to be aware of danger. I'm just waiting for Thunder and Lightning to order me to flood the earth with water.

Homer: Please go away and let me see the sun.

> Dark Cloud changes shape into that resembling a large elephant.

Dark Cloud: Look at me. I'm an elephant. I now belong to the animal world!

> Dark Cloud changes into the shape of a crocodile. Homer tries to catch Dark Cloud, but Wind blows Dark Cloud away.

Homer: What do you two want from me? I can't catch either one of you.

Dark Cloud: You can't catch me! I'm large enough to cover half the sky.

Wind: And I'm everywhere in the universe!

> Suddenly Lightning dazzles the sky. Thunder echoes all over the sky. Homer starts shaking.

Homer (terrified): What is that?

Dark Cloud (laughing derisively): You have to go back to the earth, my friend. Find a place to hide. You are in deep trouble, my little one.

> Wind groans and howls, Lightning flashes continuously, and Thunder murmurs; but Homer continues to struggle against them.

Homer (screaming): Mother! Mother! Where are you? I'm cold.

Dark Cloud (laughing): You will see more, my friend, if you don't go back to the ground.

Homer: I'm not giving up on my dream.

Wind (calming down to a gentle breeze): Listen to me, my little one. I'll tell you what I'm able to do. (In a loud and powerful voice.) I break huge trees. I flood the oceans and the seas. I destroy buildings and castles. I'm the strongest element in this universe. Do you hear me? How dare you challenge me!

> Wind blows Homer away, then blows him back. Dark Cloud becomes darker and changes its shape into many figures.

Dark Cloud (to Homer): Did you hear what Wind can do? Well, I'm able to do more. I flood rivers and lakes. I cover fields and tall trees with water. Do you think you are a match for me?

I WANT TO FLY

Wind and Dark Cloud laugh sarcastically at Homer.

Wind (to Dark Cloud): He wants to challenge both of us!

Dark Cloud drops water on Homer; Wind blows him away.

Homer: I'm wet and I'm cold ... but I will not give up flying towards the shiniest star in the universe.

Dark Cloud: If you will not change your mind and go home, I will beat you with hail and break your tiny wings and put you into a large deep lake!

Homer (proudly): I'm not afraid! I'm a duck! I can swim!

Dark Cloud: You can't swim! You're not a fish!

Homer: Maybe I'm not a fish, but I'm a good swimmer ... and a good flyer, too. Forget it! I'm not going back until I finish what I set out to do.

Dark Cloud (to Wind): My friend, we have to teach this earthly dust thing a lesson.

Homer: You may call me whatever names you wish. I'm going to fly higher and higher.

Wind (blowing gently): Nothing can fly higher than the clouds without our help.

Homer (to Wind): If you are so helpful, why are you pushing me down?

Dark Cloud (to Homer): You chose the wrong time to fly, my friend. Nature is angry with you. Go back.

Homer (insisting): No! I'm not going back. I'm going to make my dream come true. I may be young, but I'm strong. The King told me I deserve the right to fly.

Wind: How many kings have lost their kingdoms? I've destroyed many castles and palaces.

Homer (worried): Have you destroyed the Kingdom of Barnyardia?

Wind: When we are angered we have no choice. We blow down everything in our path. That is Nature's way.

Homer: I belong to Nature, too. I do what Nature has intended for me to do.

Wind: My advice to you is to go back to the earth and live in peace.

Homer: But if I have the ability to create something or to discover something in this universe, why do you and Dark Cloud want to stop me from doing it?

Wind: You're certainly stubborn. You can get into a lot of trouble by being so hardheaded!

Homer: I'm not afraid of a little trouble or hardship.

Wind: I see that I may have to ask my friend Tornado to pick you up and drop you into a desert full of snakes!

Homer: You said you were gentle. Why are you so mean now?

Wind (blowing): I told you I'm dependent on the other elements. Every element of the universe must be in harmony with every other element in order for everything to work properly.

> Dark Cloud changes its shape constantly. The sky becomes darker.

Homer: I can't see anything. Please get out of my way.

Wind (blowing gently): You will not fly any farther.

Homer: Just don't blow me away. I don't want to lose my direction.

Wind: But it's my job to blow things away. It's what I do!

Homer: Could you please blow the clouds out of my way, then?

Wind: I can't do that just because you ask for it.

Homer: Why not?

Wind: Because we all have to work together in harmony.

Homer: I'm not begging you to help me, I'm just asking you not to interfere in my plans.

Wind: Everything in this universe depends on me.

> Homer gathers his strength, then flaps his wings and flies up higher.

Homer (loudly): Yo! Ha! I see that if you want something done, you can't wait for others to do it! You have to do it yourself! I have to work hard for what I want.

Wind: You are not strong enough to get away from me.

Homer: Only one thing can stop me.

Wind: And what is that?

Homer: When I finally reach my goal. When I have done that, I will stop and look back to see where I was then and where I am now. (Homer disappears into Dark Cloud.)

Wind (loudly): I can blow you down.

Homer: You can't. I'm flying out of your reach.

Wind: Don't think you can get away from me! (To Dark Cloud.) My friend, don't let him get away. Shower him with rain, and wet his tiny wings. He doesn't have that many feathers. Then I will blow him to the North Pole where no life exists.

> Dark Cloud changes shape and starts raining heavily. Homer puts his head under his wing.

Homer: Where's this water coming from?

Dark Cloud: From me, my dear. I'm full of water. I have to pour out all the water I have. Then, if Wind blows me, I go in another direction.

> The rain comes down heavily. Wind is blowing slightly and has almost died down.

Homer (to Dark Cloud): Where is your friend Wind?

> Wind blows gently. It can be heard echoing all around.

Wind: I'm here and there, I'm everywhere. The universe can't exist without me. (To Homer.) You, my little one, look down. You see? The forest is moving. Big and small trees are dancing. The sea is roaring. Nothing can ignore me. I'm the strongest element in the universe. (To Dark Cloud.) My friend, do me a favour please, and shower this hardheaded duck until his feathers drop off from his body. Then he will fall down like a stone from the moon.

Dark Cloud: Just blow me a little bit to gather more water.

> Wind blows east and west, north and south. Dark Cloud changes shape into many figures. Homer tries to fly above Dark Cloud.

Homer: Why do you want me to go back to the earth?

Wind: Nature is angry with you, my little one. You have disobeyed one of our rules!

Homer (crying): What rules?

Wind: You said you wouldn't give up. Why are you crying now?

Homer: Because I can't see the sun.

Wind: You will never see the sun again. You are finished.

Homer: I'm not finished. I've a long way to go. I'm going to touch the sun.

He flies into Dark Cloud.

Wind (to Dark Cloud): He can still fly. Shower him with hailstones — the big ones.

Dark Cloud: I'm almost empty. I have no water left to bring him down.

Wind: Do you mean your job is done here?

Dark Cloud: I'm empty. My body is as light as a feather. Blow me to the north.

Wind: What about Homer?

Dark Cloud: Leave him alone.

Wind: If you go, he will see the sun and he'll continue his journey. Take him with you.

Clouds: When you blow me north, blow him with me.

Wind: He's getting stronger. He can fly higher and higher. He pays no attention to us. Shower him! Beat him with hail.

> The rain has stopped now, and Wind has subsided. Dark Cloud begins moving fast to the north; Homer, in the meantime, is flying with renewed energy.

Homer: Wow! Look at my wings! They're much stronger now. I can fly a long way without tiring.

Wind (blowing a bit harder): I'm the strongest element in the universe. If I can't stop this little dreamer, then I'm not as strong as I thought I was. (To Dark Cloud.) I'll blow you north. You're empty, and I can easily blow you anywhere I want.

> Wind blows Dark Cloud away, the sun comes out, and Homer flies toward the sun.

Homer (joyfully): Uh-huh! There's the sun. Oh! Lovely sun! Here I come! I'm on my way!

Wind: You're a foolish twit. You can't get rid of me that easily. I'll bring you down. I'll throw you to the ground forever. (Calling.) Where is my strong right hand? I'll prepare a battle against you the likes of which you've never seen before! (Loudly.) Homer! Homer! Come back before I lose my temper and ask Tornado to break your wings and bury you in the mud.

Homer: I don't care about Tornado! I'll fly above all the elements. Nothing can stop me!

Wind: I'll just calm down and take a deep breath to gather my strength before I blow you to the edge of the universe.

> Wind begins calming down slowly.

Homer (proudly): Yo! Ha! I should be getting close to the sun pretty soon. (He sings.)
There is no going back ... I'm aiming forward.
My mind is made up ... I'm heading for the stars.
No mountains can block my way,
Nor homesickness break my wish.

> The sky clears up, the sun shines brightly, and Wind calms down. Homer sings joyfully as he flies ever higher on his quest.

Scene Two

The sky is cloudy. The sun sends its rays through Dark Cloud. A breeze is blowing gently. Some high white clouds are moving rapidly. Homer is flying silently; only the sound of his tiny wings can be heard. Suddenly Wind starts blowing again.

Wind (loudly): This simply will not do! An insignificant duckling cannot challenge the power of a mighty wind like me! (Calling.) Homer! Homer! I told you I'd be back. Well, here I am; and I'll not allow you to fly any farther. Better for you to listen to me and go home to your mother. I don't let just anything pass through here without my permission. Do you hear me?

Homer (laughing): Look at the sun! It's so warm, my feathers have already dried up, and I'm not cold anymore. How gentle and kind the sun is. I'm going to touch it.

> Wind becomes angry, roars with displeasure, and Homer loses control for a moment.

Wind: Do you think you are stronger than anyone in this universe?

Homer: I don't know about that, but I do know that I have a strong character, and I'm smart enough to figure out a way of getting a ride from you.

Wind: Is that so? Well, I'm through being nice to you. No more Mr. Nice Guy! I will use every weapon in my arsenal to stop you. If you were really smart, you'd plan on getting a ride with Tornado. Now that's a powerful ride. It's my strongest weapon. I use it only when I'm angry.

> Wind blows strongly.

Homer: I'm no longer puny and afraid. You don't scare me a bit.

Wind (to himself): This is getting out of hand! Where is all my power? Am I losing it? Does this lamebrain have more power than I do? I've existed in this universe forever. Everyone has always been afraid of what I can do! How dare this little pipsqueak stand up to me and my friends?

> Wind increases in strength. Homer pays no attention as he struggles to fly higher.

Homer: My goal is clear. I'm thinking clearly now, and I know what I want.

> Homer flies up in a sudden burst of power. Tornado blows from the ground, creating a huge cloud of dust and rubbish. Tornado twists higher until it touches Homer and pushes him up.

Homer (bewildered): Hey! What's going on here? I'm being pushed higher … what is this?

Tornado (twisting): I am Tornado. I'm Wind's right hand. I help Wind when I'm needed.

> Homer twists and disappears into Tornado for a moment. Only his voice is heard.

Homer: I can see you, but I can't see Wind.

Tornado: When Wind gets tired or angry I am sent to take over, to break down what Wind alone cannot do. I have no compassion. All things are the same to me.

> Tornado blows strongly, moving from the earth to the sky. Homer sits on Tornado.

Homer (laughing happily): You're a good friend. I'm going higher. Keep pushing me up.

Tornado: My job is to bring you down. Just wait until I gather my full strength. I have no friends in this universe.

> Tornado becomes a dark, hissing mass of cloud. Homer disappears into Tornado again.

Homer (screaming): Oh, my eyes are full of dust. I can't see anything.

Tornado: So sorry; just doing my job. Nothing personal, you understand. I'm still only in first gear, but if you keep bothering me I'll slip into second to get you down. Now, stop and use your little brain if you want to save your life.

Homer: I will stand up to all of you. Nothing can stop me. I'll think of something.

Tornado (angrily): What're you saying, you little, funny one! What can you do?

Homer: I have a super brain. I'm thinking! I'm thinking!

> Tornado twists Homer in a wink, tossing him up and down like a straw.

Tornado (laughing): Look down. Do you see how many houses I've destroyed? How many trees have been uprooted? How many garbage cans I'm carrying? You are among this garbage. I think I'll throw everything into the ocean.

Homer: You can't throw me into the ocean. I'll outsmart you and get a ride from you.

Tornado: I will follow you wherever you go.

Homer: I'm going in only one direction.

Tornado: What direction is that?

Homer: Up towards the sun.

Tornado: I'll follow you to the sun. I'll bring you back.

Homer (to himself): What will I do? I need a plan of escape! Oh, I have to think. Think!

    Tornado gives chase as Homer attempts to escape.

Tornado: Hah! This is still only third gear. I haven't come close to using my full power yet. Because you are so little, I don't want to harm you.

    Homer is tossed around as he tries to escape. They fly around in circles, but Tornado appears to be getting the upper hand. Homer seems confused.

Homer: I've lost my sense of direction. I can't see the sun. (Screaming.) Let me go!

    Tornado calms down a little bit.

Tornado (to himself): I almost gave up. What would Wind think of me? (To Homer.) Listen, Homer, why don't you just give up and make it easier on all of us? If you don't, I'll have to use overdrive and you won't stand a chance.

Homer: I will find a way to outwit you.

Tornado: You may have the brain, but I have the power.

Homer (solicitously): Listen, my dear Tornado.

Tornado (angrily): What?

Homer: Let's make a deal.

Tornado: What deal?

Homer: You be gentle with me and I will not oppose you. We have to make peace.

Tornado drops to the ground. Homer grabs this opportunity and flies away!

Tornado (loudly): You can't get away from me. I'm so tall I can reach the stars.

Homer: But you can't reach me!

Homer flies higher. Tornado follows, twisting and turning, trying to catch him.

Tornado (exhausted): That's my limit! I've had it! I can't blow any higher!

Homer is now flying high above Tornado.

Homer: The more you blow, the higher I go!

Tornado: I'll get you!

Tornado blows up and down, west and east, but Homer appears to be safe.

Homer: I can see the sun now!

Tornado: Looks like my job here is over. I'm heading to the desert. I have to carry all this rubbish and deposit it somewhere.

Homer: You're too late, Tornado. I got away! You can't go higher than the horizon.

Tornado (to himself): What happened to me? I'm dying! I'm the only element of nature that never gives up! How could a tiny creature like that get away from me? How humiliating. I'll never live this down. I'm dying! I'm dying!

As Tornado dies down, the sky clears up and the sun appears. Homer is flying happily.

Homer: I'm thirsty, and I'm hungry; but I'm not tired.

From far away, Dark Cloud moves towards Homer. The sun disappears.

Homer: The clouds are coming again. I have to fly higher to avoid them.

Dark Cloud approaches Homer quietly.

Dark Cloud: I have come to save your life. I'm a friendly cloud. Open your mouth.

Homer: You have some water?

Dark Cloud: I have a lot.

Homer: I need only a small mouthful.

Homer opens his mouth and water drops from Dark Cloud.

Homer: Enough! I asked for a drink, not a bath. Please stop!

Dark Cloud: But I'm helping you.

Homer: Thank you, but I have enough water; besides, you've hidden the sun from me.

Dark Cloud: Well, don't call for water again!

Homer: Just leave me! Go away!

Wind starts to blow. Dark Cloud moves away.

Dark Cloud (to Homer): Good luck with Wind, Homer!

Homer: Why don't you tell Wind to leave me alone?

Dark Cloud: Because Wind controls almost everything. Look, I'm being blown away.

Wind blows Dark Cloud away, and the sky clears up.

Wind: Well, here I am again. Are you still flying? The clouds are weak.

Look how easily I blew them away. Tornado is still working on the ground. He will be back.

Homer: Why is every element against me? What have I done wrong? Why aren't you kind and helpful like King Mortimer? It's not too hard for you to blow me up towards the sun.

Wind: I can't. My job is to blow east, west, north, south, and down. Besides, the elements don't like any smarty-pants challenging their authority or power.

Homer nervously opens and folds his wings.

Homer: Look how my wings have developed; I'm strong enough to fly very high.

Wind (laughing): You're just dreaming! You are not far away from the earth. Look down!

Homer looks down, then flies up.

Homer: I will fly higher. Please, stop pushing me down.

Wind: Don't think we're weak just because we're gentle! We just don't want to harm you.

Homer (defiantly): I'm not afraid of you or any of the elements. I want to touch the sun!

Wind (sarcastically): You're in luck today. I'll let you fly a little higher because I'm going to the North Pole; but when I get back, you'd better be ready to go home. Good-bye. I'm going now.

Wind dies down slowly. The sky clears up. Homer sings as he flies toward the sun.

Homer (singing):
Don't say "I can't…"
Nothing in the world's impossible to be;

Always say "I hope."
Don't say "It's too late…"
Nothing in the world's impossible to see;
Always say "I wish."
Day by day the far-away comes nearer
If you say, "Just keep on trying."
Don't break your faith; don't lose your dream;
Don't give your hope away!

As Homer continues his journey to the sun, his voice fades away into the distance.

Scene Three

The sky above the mountains on the distant horizon is a clear blue. In the distance to one side, Dark Cloud can be seen coming closer. Slowly and relentlessly, Dark Cloud develops into a strong, whirling, tumbling mass of potential danger. The sun appears and disappears as Dark Cloud forms and reforms. Homer is oblivious to all this development and continues merrily flying toward the sun.

Homer (feebly): Oh! Mother! Mother! (He looks at the sun.) What a lovely gold medal that makes! If I could only fly around the sun, I'd be a champion and a hero. I could claim that gold medal for my own! My ambition and desire are strong, but my poor wings are not. I'll have to fly much higher to reach the sun. (The sun disappears into Dark Cloud, but its rays still shine through from time to time.) Don't go, please. I'm coming. (He flies with increased enthusiasm, but he soon tires.) I can't fly anymore. Who will help me? Is there someone or something that can help me? Oh, my wings are tired. Please, someone, anyone, help me.

Wind starts blowing gently.

Wind: I'm back. I'm the magic wind.

Tornado gets up from the ground, reaching skyward.

Tornado: Me too, I'm back. (To Wind.) I'm ready to bring this smart alec down to earth.

Dark Cloud comes down from above. All three surround Homer.

Homer (frightened): What do you want from me? I will not surrender to any of you.

Wind: We are three and you are one. We control the universe. (To Dark Cloud.) Pour him with all that you have.

Dark Cloud changes shape and envelopes Homer.

Dark Cloud: I feel sorry for this creature. I think I'll keep my water for another place.

Wind (to Dark Cloud): If we don't show our strength to this small creature, our reputations as powerful elements will be destroyed. We have to be tough with our enemies.

Dark Cloud: He's not an enemy.

Wind: But he keeps defying us. He wants to show he can overcome our powers.

Dark Cloud: He has no power to defeat us.

Wind (to Tornado): Bring him down.

Tornado: I tried, but I can't. He just won't give up.

Wind: Use your power to blow him away. Take him to the desert.

Dark Cloud (to Wind): We've done all we can in this place. It's time we moved on.

Wind (angrily): You both are in my power. You have to obey my orders. (To Dark Cloud.) I'll blow you back to cover the sun. Don't let him see the sky.

Dark Cloud: It's too late. We have to move on. That's Nature's way.

Wind: We must show this pea-brain our power, to let him know we can make a difference in this universe.

Dark Cloud (to Wind): We have to respect the laws of Nature, my friend. Everything in this universe has to come to an end, and my end is near. I'm going.

Wind: You can't go.

> Dark Cloud moves west. Wind blows it back. They struggle against each other.

Dark Cloud (angrily): I will not release any drops of rain on him.

Wind: Where is Tornado?

> Tornado boils up from the ground in a sudden rush toward the sky.

Tornado: I'm here!

Wind: Why did you go down to the ground?

Tornado: Well, Dark Cloud was going to rain, so I died down.

Wind: Dark Cloud won't rain.

Tornado: Then I will not blow the little creature away.

Wind: You both are a disgrace to Nature. Get away from here! Where is Homer?

Tornado: He's high above me, out of reach. I couldn't catch him.

Wind (yelling): You are both useless elements. (To Dark Cloud.) I won't let you go. (Wind blows strongly.) Cover him from above. (To Tornado.) You, Tornado, calm down and go back to the ground at a lower level.

> Tornado slows down and drops to the ground. Dark Cloud is above Homer and starts to rain. Homer appears between Dark Cloud and Tornado, struggling against Wind.

Wind (laughing): I've got you now, Homer!

Homer (to Dark Cloud): Why are you raining on me?

Dark Cloud: Wind forced me to rain.

Homer: Please go away with your water.

Dark Cloud: I want to, but Wind won't let me.

Wind (to Dark Cloud): I want you to pour water on him until his feathers drop from his body. Then I will throw him to the ground. (To Tornado.) And you, my fellow Tornado! Take his body and shatter it into pieces of rotting flesh and throw him into an ocean full of hungry fish. Then we will celebrate the end of this would-be Nature-conqueror!

Homer (screaming): No, you can't do that to me.

Wind (blowing wildly): You want to see more of my power? Where is my great magic Lightning? Come, come in a flash! (Lightning strikes the sky several times.) You will see more, my little one. (The blowing increases.) Where is the most powerful voice in the universe? Come, Thunder, and let your voice echo all over the earth and sky. (Thunder rumbles from all around.)

Homer (screaming): Leave me alone! Why are you punishing me like this?

Wind (blowing): Here is some more for you! Look at the sky!

> Homer looks up as huge hailstones come from Dark Cloud. He puts his head beneath his wings.

Homer (screaming): Oh! My head! What is this? I'm cold.

Wind (laughing): Down! Down! This is Hail. It will break your wings.

Homer: I told you nothing could or would stop me. I'm not afraid of your power.

Wind (blowing just a bit nervously now): Then what kind of power do you have?

Homer: My power is in mind over matter. I can think, and I think you are not as powerful as you'd like to be. You can be overcome.

Homer struggles to fly away.

Wind (to himself): Am I not the most powerful element in the universe?

> Wind howls and roars. Dark Cloud becomes very dark; hail drops continuously. Lightning strikes the sky, and Thunder rumbles. Homer is heard screaming for help amid all these other sounds of Nature.

> After several minutes of this turmoil, the lines of Rainbow appear in the background just beyond the mountains. As Rainbow gets brighter, the sounds diminish until everything is deathly still. Rainbow climbs higher until it reaches Homer. Homer is frightened at this new phenomenon.

Homer: What is this? Who is carrying me? (He looks down.) These colours — they're beautiful! They must be heaven's rays. (Joyfully.) I almost got a ride from the clouds. (He stops suddenly.) Wait a minute. ... Who or what are you? What are you trying to do to me?

Rainbow: I am Rainbow. I heard you call for help, so I came to see what I could do.

Wind (to Rainbow): Nobody can help him now. He is our enemy. He wants to be the most powerful one in the universe.

Rainbow (rising higher): We don't have enemies in this universe, my friend!

Wind: Are you saying you will help him reach his destination?

Rainbow: Why not? The universe is vast. If this little being can accomplish something, let him do it, provided that he doesn't destroy any part of our environment.

Homer (eagerly): No, no. I certainly would not destroy anything in nature. I just want to make my dream come true, and discover those things that are still unknown.

Wind (to Rainbow): And what about us? Can we exist if we are shown to be weak?

Rainbow: We will exist as long as Nature allows us to be a part of it.

Wind: It's a disgrace to be bettered by such an insignificant creature.

Rainbow (pushing Homer up): His body may be small but his thoughts and deeds are big.

> Homer is on top of Rainbow. His feathers reflect the colours of the rainbow. Wind calms down, briefly, then begins to blow strongly.

Wind (angrily): You have to understand, my friend Rainbow, if that puny creature gets control, our very existence will be in his hands. We will lose our independence, and forever be at his mercy! I'm not giving up. I will fight for my personal existence and freedom.

> Wind blows, clinking and clanging all over the sky. Rainbow bursts up into Dark Cloud, with Homer still on top flying comfortably.

Rainbow (gently to Wind): Calm down, my friend. Don't be foolish. We're all part of this universe. We have to be kind and helpful to all creatures. This puny creature, as you call him, has the right to do what he can!

Wind (angrily): I'll bring him down. He has no right to challenge us.

Rainbow: It will be difficult to bring him down because you are using physical force and little Homer is using willpower and faith in himself.

Wind (blowing severely): I'm the strongest unseen power in the universe. I will use all my powers at once to bring him down. (Boastfully.) I'm the most powerful element in the universe! (This last utterance is heard echoing all 'round.)

Rainbow (to Homer): Listen, little one! I cannot help you for very long.

Homer: Why not?

Rainbow (quietly): Because Wind is very angry. He's calling on all his powers. You'll have to decide whether you want to fly farther or not.

Homer (loudly): Of course I want to fly farther. I'm determined to fly to the sun.

Rainbow (proudly): I will do my best to help you.

Homer: I appreciate your help, my friend Rainbow!

> The lines of Rainbow become more colourful and dazzling. Rays of sunlight glitter through Dark Cloud. Homer sits on top of Rainbow, getting higher and higher. Wind blows from all directions.

Wind: (to Rainbow): My fellow Rainbow, I will banish you from this universe forever.

Rainbow (calmly): My kindness and gentleness keep me in existence in this universe. I will put this little one as high as I can, to save him from pitiless and unkind elements like you.

Wind (roaring): Where are my other powers? Where are Lightning and Thunderstorm? (Blowing.) Do you hear me? I beg Mother Nature to give me one last chance to bring this usurper down and throw him to the ground.

> Wind has calmed to a murmur now; Lightning splits the sky, and Thunder throbs. Beyond the hills the sky lights up for a brief instant, then becomes very dark. Again Homer disappears into the darkness. Only his voice is heard.

Homer (to Rainbow): Please, push me higher so I can see the sun.

Rainbow (gently): Take it easy. You will see the sun tomorrow, if you fly all night.

Homer: Thank you. I will.

Wind (dejectedly): It looks like my time is up. I'm gone with the sunset. (To Homer.) How did you manage to get away from me? I'm dying with the sunset! I have no strength left. I'm dying! (Wind calms down to a gentle breeze, then stops altogether.)

Rainbow (to Homer): Don't think that you are out of danger yet! Look to the west, you see? There's a big cloud coming again.

Homer (terrified): Please, push me above the clouds so I can see the sun. I will follow it.

Rainbow: You have to fly east to avoid the clouds. By this time tomorrow you will see the sun rising from the east.

Homer (sadly): The sun is gone.

Rainbow: Don't worry about the sun. When the earth has finished its daily orbit, the sun will rise again. It will set and rise every day. The clouds are coming. It's already starting to rain. There will be a heavy rain after I leave.

Homer: Where are you going?

Rainbow: My mission is over. There's nothing more for me to do. I have to go.

Homer (begging): Please, my colourful friend, stay with me until tomorrow morning.

Rainbow: Oh, I can't do that. That would be against Nature's laws. My time is limited. Good luck, little Homer!

Rainbow paints the sky with colourful lines and disappears.

Homer (loudly): Please, don't leave. I need you. … Where are you?

> Dark Cloud moves so fast that its edge almost touches
> Homer's right wing. Heavy rain is heard. Homer instinctively
> runs away in the opposite direction from Dark Cloud. The
> sky becomes very dark. Homer disappears for a short time.
> Dark Cloud passes by. The sky clears up. Some stars appear
> in the sky. Homer appears flying and singing.

Homer (singing):
I'm a flyer now.
No night's darkness can scare me;
No night's loneliness stops me — my path is clear.
In darkness or in light, I will follow it to the stars.

ACT TWO
Scene One

Night has descended. Everything is still. The sky is clear and full of bright stars. A full moon rises above the hills. Moonlight reflects off Homer's feathers as he slowly flies through the darkness.

Homer (to himself): I feel so strong! (He looks down.) I can't see anything. It's so dark down there. How far I seem to be from the earth. (He looks up to the stars.) The sky is filled with stars. I believe I can make it to the sun! My wings have become strong enough to fly all night. Tomorrow I will be close to the sun. Yo! Ha!

> In the distance a voice is heard calling. It is Nigel Pigeon, Homer's friend. He is searching for Homer.

Nigel (calling): Homer! Homer! Are you listening? Don't try to fly in the darkness.

> Homer stops for a moment, looks down briefly, then looks up again.

Homer (surprised): Who's calling me? Am I still close to the earth? (He speeds up.) I want to be high, close to the stars.

Nigel: Homer! Please come back. We all miss you.

Homer (to himself): No, I'm not going back. I'm not listening to anyone. Oh! Wait a minute! Maybe I'm just dreaming. It's not a real voice. It's only an illusion! Nobody could fly this high! (He laughs loudly.) Yo! Ha!

The sky becomes brighter. The full moon rises, and Homer continues his joyful flight.

Nigel (worried): That was quite the storm last night! Do you think Homer survived it?

Priscilla (a bit apprehensively): I don't know! It would be a miracle if he did!

Nigel (sadly): I really hope nothing bad happened to him.

Priscilla (almost in despair): I doubt if anyone could survive such a strong storm.

Nigel (hopefully): Well we have to look for him. We have to find him, dead or alive.

Priscilla: Where do you think he could be?

Nigel (proudly): He was always very good at avoiding bad things. I think he's still alive.

Priscilla (desperately): We won't be able to see him in this darkness!

Nigel: He couldn't have flown very far. He's probably somewhere just above us.

Priscilla (looks down): Maybe we should look for him in the forest. Wind may have blown him against some tree trunk, and he may be lying hurt somewhere.

Nigel (calling): Homer! Homer!

Priscilla: Let's go back to Barnyardia.

Nigel: Not yet. Let's look just a little bit longer.

Priscilla: Nigel, I'm so scared.

Nigel: Scared of what?

Priscilla: Of the darkness.

> They look at each other for a moment. Then suddenly Priscilla huddles very close to Nigel in fright.

Nigel: What's wrong with you?

Priscilla: I feel so afraid.

Nigel (laughing): Don't be afraid, Priscilla! Look at the sky — see how bright the stars are. Look at the moon — it's smiling at us. (Gently.) We have to find Homer. It will be the best gift that we could ever give his mother.

Priscilla (still frightened): What if we come to some harm? Who will save us?

Nigel: There are two of us. We can help each other.

Priscilla: I'm still afraid!

> Priscilla attempts to turn back. Nigel blocks her way.

Nigel: Don't be a coward! Let's fly just a little bit higher. We will find him.

Priscilla: I'm not an adventurer. I don't like to put my life in danger for some stranger.

Nigel: Homer's not a stranger. He's part of our lives. We all live in this world to help each other. Please, Priscilla, let's fly a little farther. We can make Mother Mathilda very happy.

Priscilla (nervously): It's too dark to fly any farther. Let's go back. (Loudly.) I'm afraid!

Nigel (quietly): Don't shout so loudly. You'll scare Homer.

Priscilla (nervously): I think he's lying hurt somewhere. He couldn't possibly fly so long.

Nigel: I'm sure he's somewhere in the air. He's very strong and determined.

Priscilla (angrily): I think he's on the ground, maybe somewhere stuck in a mud hole.

Nigel: No, he's not in a mud hole. He's flying in the air.

Priscilla: Do you think he's still alive?

Nigel (eagerly): Yes, he's still alive. We have to find him and take him back to his mother. Let's fly faster, before he gets tired and crashes to earth.

Priscilla (angrily): I don't want to sacrifice my life for your precious Homer.

Nigel (calmly): That's what life's about. He's our friend. Sometimes we have to sacrifice ourselves for our friends. He's just a dreamer. (He pushes Priscilla up.) Come on, Priscilla, don't you feel sorry for his mother?

Priscilla (getting away from Nigel): Why don't we wait until tomorrow morning? Then everything will be clear. If he's flying we can see him.

Nigel: Tomorrow may be too late to save his life.

Priscilla (nervously): I will not fly any farther. I'm going back.

Nigel (begging): Please, do it for me.

Priscilla: Begging won't do any good. I'm going back.

Nigel: Then do it for Mathilda's sake!

Priscilla: What do you mean?

Nigel: Wouldn't you like to see Homer's mother smiling happily?

Priscilla: It's dangerous to fly in the darkness. We've never flown at night before.

Nigel: We've never had a reason to before, but we do now. We have to save a friend.

Priscilla: I'm cold. I'm going back.

> Priscilla flaps her wings, then straightens her body and heads downward. Nigel follows her.

Nigel: Priscilla! Wait a minute! Come back. Don't be so heartless! Please come back!

> Nigel catches Priscilla and pulls her up. They struggle briefly.

Priscilla (screaming): Let me go! … Let me go! … I'm afraid!

Nigel: You're a coward!

> Suddenly Homer's voice is heard singing. Nigel and Priscilla listen to the voice.

Homer's voice (singing):
I'm a flyer now.
My path is drawn with silver and gold.
I'm a flyer now,
No night's darkness can scare me.

Nigel (proudly): It's Homer. He's always singing. He's alive! … He's alive! And he's not far away from us. (Calling.) Homer! Homer! (He pulls Priscilla up.) Let's go. We have to find him.

Priscilla (thankfully): I can't believe it! How can he fly in this darkness and be so happy?

Nigel: He's a courageous one.

Priscilla: He doesn't think. That's why he likes adventures.

Nigel (proudly): He has already achieved something. He wasn't able to fly before. Look at how he flies now. That's progress! Do you see him? He's flying like an eagle!

Both of them look at Homer in the far distance in amazement.

Priscilla: I can't believe my eyes! He's grown up!

They stop for a moment and look down.

Nigel: Let's get him back, before he gets harmed.

Nigel pulls Priscilla up, with difficulty.

Priscilla: What if he refuses to go back?

Nigel (impatiently): Let's go! … He won't refuse us. He's probably very tired and hungry.

Priscilla: Don't tell me he's tired and hungry! Look how he's flying. He's full of energy!

Homer is singing. Nigel and Priscilla listen and dance joyfully.

Homer's voice (singing):
I'm a flyer now;
My path leads me to the highest.
I'm a flyer now;
My goal is within my reach.

Nigel (cheerfully): He's an angel flying in the moonlight. We have to bring him back. His voice seems so weak. Let's get him before he collapses to the ground.

They flap their wings three times and burst upwards into the sky. The sky becomes brighter. The sound of flapping wings echoes everywhere, and slowly recedes as the pair fly upward towards Homer's singing voice.

Scene Three

It is late into the night; the full moon travels silently to its rendezvous. The sky is filled with countless twinkling stars, completely unconcerned with the shadowy figure flying ever so slowly now. Suddenly Nigel and Priscilla surround Homer closely.

Homer (scared): Oh! No! Who are you?

Nigel: Don't be afraid, we've come to take you home.

Homer (surprised): Oh! Nigel! … and Priscilla! How could you ever fly so high?

Nigel: We can probably fly higher yet, but we have to go back. Your mother is waiting for you.

Homer: My mother? (Proudly.) Does my mother know I'm flying?

Nigel: Yes, she knows, but she wants you back.

    Homer struggles to get away from them.

Homer: No, I'm not going back. I want to get closer to the sun by tomorrow morning. My mother will be proud of me.

    Homer struggles to fly up. He flaps his wings strongly.

Nigel: You're tired. You're very lucky you survived the storms.

Homer: I fought against all the elements. It wasn't easy getting a ride from Wind!

Nigel (calmly): Bravo! Bravo! But now we have to go back.

    Homer struggles to get away from them. Nigel and

Priscilla encircle him and head down toward the ground with him.

Homer (struggling): Leave me alone. I'm not going back.

Nigel: Don't be silly! Homer! Don't you love your mother?

Homer: Of course I do — very much.

Nigel: So, why not go back to her?

Homer (struggling): After I touch the sun I will go back to her.

Nigel: My dear Homer! You've a long ways to go yet. You're not far from the earth.

Homer (still struggling): I'm close to the stars. I could reach them, but I want the brightest star in this universe. I want to touch the sun!

Nigel: Homer! You are only dreaming.

Homer struggles to get rid of them.

Priscilla (to Nigel): We can't force him to come back if he doesn't want to.

Nigel: Just keep trying gently.

Homer pushes Nigel away, then flaps his wings in the eyes of Priscilla and flies away.

Priscilla (screaming): Oh! My eyes. I can't see! I'll get you for this, Homer! Just you wait! I'll get you!

She reaches him and tries to get him back. Homer flaps his wings again and again in the eyes of Priscilla and gets rid of her.

Homer (proudly): Nothing can stop me.

Priscilla (calling): Nigel! Nigel! Where are you? I can't see. Oh, my eyes! Let's go back.

Nigel helps Priscilla and guides her. Homer flies far away from them.

Nigel: What happened to your eyes?

Priscilla (wiping her eyes): He flapped his wings in both my eyes. He has strong wings. I can't believe it! Let's go back. I can't open my eyes. Let's leave him and go back.

Nigel: Wait a minute.

Nigel looks at Priscilla's eyes.

Priscilla (screaming): Oh! My eyes! I'm not going after this idiot anymore. Let's go back.

Nigel (calling): Homer! Homer! We're going back! (To Priscilla.) He's disappeared! What'll we tell his mother?

Priscilla (screaming): I'm in pain — my eyes! Let's go back.

Nigel puts one wing around Priscilla and they head toward the ground. The sky is clear and full of bright stars. The full moon continues traveling toward its morning rendezvous. Homer appears far away flying and singing.

Homer (singing):
The night seems so long; the stars seem so far...
No matter if the night is endless;
No darkness makes me hopeless.
With the bright stars guiding, I'm flying so high.
Past the moon I will soon be going;
Waiting for the golden sun to break the darkness
And achieve what my mother thinks is right for her son.

Homer's voice echoes throughout. Three big, bright stars around the full moon send their beams to shine on Homer as he continues flying higher until he disappears from sight.

End of Part II

Part Three

Journey Through Space

Homer has now reached the second phase of his dream by overcoming the elements of nature. Neither strong wind nor tornado nor fierce rain could make him veer from his determined path.

In Part III, "Journey through Space," he will meet with even stronger foes. He will be tempted by the various planets to stop and stay with them, either temporarily or even permanently. Will he be able to resist the temptation?

Read "A Duckling's Dream," Part III, "Journey through Space," to find out!

The dream develops...

In Part I, "A Duckling's Dream," we met Homer, an ambitious and determined duckling. His one dream was to fly to the sun. He met and overcame many obstacles on his quest. With the support of his young friends and the supernatural powers of the king of Barnyardia, Homer eventually realized the beginning of his dream he could fly! As Part I ended, Homer was on his way, flying to the sun.

In Part II, "Against the Odds," Homer met even more formidable opponents. The elements of Nature took exception to his exploits and banded together to stop his foolhardiness. Homer took on the challenges of Nature's powerful elements as he continued his journey to the sun. Who would be the ultimate victor in this titanic struggle? Was Nature powerful enough to stop a young duckling's dream? Or was determination and willpower enough to overcome all hardships? Homer eventually succeeded because he was determined to get what he had set his heart on. Despite the anger of the wild wind and the other elements, Homer was able to continue his journey.

In Part III, "Journey through Space," Homer has grown into a fine young drake, and he continues his quest on a dark night full of bright stars. Will the stars let him continue his flight to the sun? Maybe not! The Moon wants Homer to live with him. The planets Venus, Mercury, and Mars also want Homer to live with them and discover what they have to offer.

Will Homer give up his dream for the adventure of living on another planet? Read on to find out what Homer's decision and new role will be.

The Characters

Homer	a duckling
Mathilda	a duck, Homer's mother
Nigel	a male pigeon
Priscilla	a female pigeon
King Mortimer	a turkey tom, king of Barnyardia
Sylvester	a cat, King Mortimer's chief advisor
Jeremiah	a young cockerel
Penelope	a pullet
Bartholomew	a male gosling
Prunella	a female gosling
Moon	a gray heavenly body
Venus	a yellow planet
Mercury	a silver-blue planet
Mars	a red planet

Setting

The action in Act One takes place in space at night.

Prologue

The Kingdom of Barnyardia after the storm. It is past midnight. The royal castle is silhouetted against the dark sky. The ground is littered with leaves and broken branches. A lone tree stands out against the sky, its trunk shattered, but its top still intact. The clear sky is full of bright stars. A full moon rises on its journey across the sky. King Mortimer sits on the tree trunk, looking at the stars through a telescope. Mathilda Duck, sitting beside him, searches the sky eagerly. Penelope Chicken and Prunella Goose sit around King Mortimer, looking at him curiously. Jeremiah Chicken and Bartholomew Goose wander about aimlessly.

Mathilda (nervously): Where are they? Why is it taking them so long to come back?

Penelope (to Mathilda): Who are you looking for, Mother Mathilda?

Mathilda: I'm looking for Homer. King Mortimer said he sent Nigel and Priscilla Pigeon to bring him back. (She looks around nervously.) It's been a long time since they left. I doubt Homer flew very far. They should have caught up to him by now.

King Mortimer (shouting excitedly): I found it! I found it!

> Mathilda jumps up and almost lands on King Mortimer's back.

Mathilda (joyfully): He's alive! He's alive! My son is flying. …

> Penelope and Prunella climb onto the tree trunk and try looking through the telescope.

Penelope: I want to see Homer! I want to see him flying!

Prunella (calling loudly and waving): Homer! Here we are! Come back! We want you home.

> Jeremiah and Bartholomew look at the sky, then join King Mortimer on the tree trunk.

Mathilda: I want my son back now. He's shown us he can fly. That's enough for him.

Jeremiah: I want to see him. Where is he?

Bartholomew (to the king): Could I learn to fly like Homer? (He pushes Jeremiah away.) I want to see Homer. I want to see how he flaps his wings.

> King Mortimer moves away from the telescope and turns to Mathilda.

King Mortimer: I only found a new star. I didn't see Homer anywhere in the sky.

> All look at King Mortimer, disappointment clear on their faces.

Mathilda: What's that you're saying? (She pauses.) ... You were just looking for a new star?

King Mortimer: Yes, a new star. It will be added to the other stars.

> They all look up at the sky silently.

Mathilda: The sky is full of stars! I want my son back.

> King Mortimer looks again through the telescope.

King Mortimer: Oh! Look! There's Mercury!

> They crowd around him, all trying to get a look through the telescope at the same time. Mathilda stays away. She gazes at the sky nervously.

Jeremiah (in amazement): Mercury! What is Mercury? I've never heard of it before.

King Mortimer: There are many stars in space. Some of them are very close to our planet. Here! Come take a look.

> Jeremiah comes to the telescope and looks through it at the stars.

Mathilda (to Jeremiah): You have to find Homer! Look towards the east. Perhaps the wind blew him to the east. (She points to the east.)

Jeremiah (awed): Wow! Just look at that, will you!

> Mathilda turns to Jeremiah and attempts to look through the telescope.

Mathilda: He's flying? Can you see him? Let me look.

Jeremiah (looking through the telescope): That's so beautiful.

Penelope: What is it?

Jeremiah (still looking): It's a huge ball moving very fast.

Penelope: Let me see it.

Jeremiah (still looking): This is really exciting! Look how fast it's moving; I can't follow it.

> He moves the telescope, attempting to pursue the star.

Penelope: Let me look, too! I want to see Homer!

> She pushes Jeremiah away, seizes the telescope, and looks through it.

Mathilda (to King Mortimer): Do you think my son could fly all night in this darkness?

King Mortimer (hesitantly): Perhaps! ... Maybe! ... Oh, I don't know! It has been so long!

Mathilda: What do you mean?

King Mortimer: I'm just guessing, but I think he's still flying around out there somewhere.

Mathilda: I don't want him to fly far away from home. I'm already proud of him, but at the same time I'm angry with him because he left me alone.

Penelope (shouting): It's him! It's Homer! He's flying very fast. He's going higher and higher. (She reaches out to Mathilda.) Come take a look at your son.

Mathilda goes to the telescope and looks through it.

King Mortimer (to Penelope): You are sure it was him?

Penelope (hardly able to hold back her excitement): Yes. It's him. It was Homer. I'm sure it was.

King Mortimer: By himself? Flying alone without the help of Nigel and Priscilla Pigeon?

Mathilda (peering through the telescope): My son! Homer! He's flying. I want him back. I can see him close to the stars. He's not far away from that big star.

King Mortimer (laughing): He's not really that close. It just looks that way through the telescope! We can see only the closest planets, like Mercury, Venus, and Mars.

Mathilda continues searching with the telescope.

Mathilda (worried): I want my son back. I don't want him to go to another planet. We have a nice home here on this planet.

King Mortimer takes Mathilda aside. Bartholomew looks through the telescope.

Bartholomew: Where is he?

Jeremiah (to Bartholomew): Do you think he could make it to the sun?

Bartholomew: I don't know. I can't see him! He's disappeared! (He looks around the sky for a short time, then fixes on a spot.) Boy! Look at that, would you! It's a bright ball of clouds moving slowly! But where is Homer? I don't see him.

Jeremiah: Maybe he's behind the ball!

> Bartholomew and Jeremiah join Mathilda. King Mortimer goes to the telescope and makes some adjustments. Then he looks through it at the stars.

Bartholomew (to Mathilda): Homer has disappeared again.

Mathilda (to King Mortimer): Can you see my son?

King Mortimer (excited): I can see many stars and I can identify most of them. (Moving the telescope around, he stops and studies the sky.) There's the red planet. It's Mars!

Mathilda: Do you mean my son is close to Mars?

King Mortimer: No, I don't see Homer. (He straightens himself and ponders.) If he dreamed about stars like Mars ... hmm. ... (He pauses.) Maybe his dream can come true; but he dreamed about the sun. It's hard to take his foolish dream seriously. (He calls again to Jeremiah.) Jeremiah! Come take a look at Mars.

> Jeremiah looks through the telescope. King Mortimer goes back to Mathilda.

Mathilda: My son was so serious about what he was doing.

Jeremiah (jumping up and down): Oh, look! It's him! He's back! I see two things flying side by side. They're coming towards us. (Loudly.) It's Homer! Homer's coming back.

Mathilda (joyfully): He's back. My son's back. I hope he's safe. I want him unharmed.

> Mathilda kneels down on the ground and looks at the sky. The others surround her.

King Mortimer (to Mathilda): He's back. Don't worry.

Mathilda (singing):
Lord on high, I prayed day and night for my son.
Lord on high, hear my weak voice before my heart breaks down.
Lord on high, bring my son home; I need him soon.

All together (singing):
Lord on high, bring Homer home. We need him soon.
Lord on high, bring Homer home.

Mathilda (singing): Lord on high, bring my son home.

> He's a dreamer. He's so little. Bring him home.

All together (singing): Lord on high, bring him home. Bring him soon.

> Nigel and Priscilla have already landed on the tree trunk. Mathilda rushes to them.

Mathilda: Where is my son?

Nigel (sadly): He refused to come. He insisted on flying to the sun. He's still flying out there somewhere — higher and higher on his way to the sun.

> All look at the sky with fear and raise their hands to pray for the safety of Homer.

All together (singing):
Lord on high, bring him home. We need him soon.
Lord on high, bring Homer home.

> A thick fog moves in and slowly engulfs everything. The singing voices fade.

ACT ONE
Scene One

The fog is everywhere. It clears slowly, and the sky appears very clear but dark. Bright stars appear, twinkling. The Moon has almost set. The Milky Way can be seen clearly descending like a waterfall across the sky. Everything is quiet except for the sound of Homer's wings flapping from far away. The rhythm of the beating wings slows down, and we hear the sound of Homer's breathing mixed in with the sound of his wings. The sounds get louder until Homer bursts onto the scene, his feathers reflecting the golden light of the Moon. Above him, fragments of meteorites float in the air, crashing against each other, sending out sparks of light and making croaking and clanking sounds. Homer sees the rock fragments coming toward him, and he dodges them as they drop from the Moon's surface.

Homer (frightened): What is this? What's going on? Is the sky raining rocks? (A small fragment of rock drops on him.) Ouch! That hurts! The sky is clear. Where is this hail coming from?

> A ray of gray light bursts from the Moon and spotlights Homer.

Moon (gently): Hello, I hope I didn't frighten you. I am your neighbour, Moon. You are heading to the sun, as I understand it.

Homer (proudly): Yes, but how do you know that?

Moon: Oh, there are a lot of things that I know. I am part of the universe.

> Fragments of rocks are still floating around Homer, making a brilliant light.

Homer: Where do these rocks come from? Why are they falling on me?

Moon: I'm angry with you.

Homer (with amazement): Why? You have always been so quiet and gentle. Why are you angry with me?

Moon: Because, Homer, you have disappointed me.

Homer: Why are you angry? How have I disappointed you?

Moon: A long time ago, when you were still quite young, you used to sit and watch me for hours before you went to sleep. You used to dream about what I was like. You even wished someday to be able to touch me. Now you have your chance, and you seem to ignore me.

Homer: I have a goal to achieve. I'm flying to the sun. I have no time to talk to you.

Moon: I'm better than the sun. I have everything that you wish to achieve.

Homer: You're not as bright as the sun. I'm not going to land on you. Stop interfering with my dream.

Moon: Put aside that silly notion. Stay with me. You can achieve many things with me.

Homer: Like what?

Moon: Like a very fulfilling life.

Homer: No. ... But thank you for the offer anyway.

Moon: How can you refuse my offer?

Homer: It's simple: you are not on my agenda. I will not change my goal for your sake.

Moon (angrily): Then I will not let you fly any further. I feel ignored here among the planets. (Loudly.) I am the Moon. I will give you something worthwhile if you stay here with me. I will give you a rewarding life.

> Homer tries to avoid the light and the rocks as the conversation continues.

Homer: Stop that! Stop shining your light on me and throwing rocks. That hurts.

Moon: Don't try to escape. One little move from me and you will be thrown to the ground and covered with huge rocks. You made me angry and I have no pity for two-timing, fair-weather friends!

> The sound of crashing rocks echoes all over the sky.

Homer (frightened): What have I done to you to deserve this kind of treatment?

Moon (loudly): Watch out! Here comes another one!

> Fragments of rocks fly all around Homer.

Homer: Please, don't hurt me.

Moon: Do you think I'm useless in the universe? Powerless? Well, you're wrong.

Homer (begging): Just leave me alone.

Moon: I want to be a useful heavenly body. I want to sustain life on my soil. You could make a good life on me. You are a bright young man, Homer. Think about it! Create a life on me. I'm big enough to carry millions of others like you.

Homer: Why don't you just stay quiet as always and be content with your present life. ... And leave me alone. My dream is about much more important things. Like the bright stars, for example.

Moon (angrily): Stop talking about the sun!

Homer (angrily): And you stop interfering with my dream. Who is the brightest and most powerful body in this universe?

Moon: But I have power, too. I help make the universe what it is.

> Moon's rays twist and bend in all directions uncontrollably. The sound of crashing rocks is heard all over the sky. Then a flood of rocks drops over Homer.

Homer (screaming): You are not the same gentle moon that I once knew. You were kind, then. What's changed you into such an aggressive member of the universe?

Moon: Everything in this universe has to fight to remain alive. It's the law of Nature.

Homer: Then I must fight to keep my dream. Without it, I am nothing. I have no purpose in this universe. To live without trying to achieve my goal is no life at all. Neither you nor anyone nor anything else will deter me from my path.

Moon: I can help you achieve a meaningful life. Stay with me and see what glories are in store for you.

Homer: I can't.

Moon: Then I will beat you into a small pile of dust!

Homer: You can't stop me! I'm going to the sun!

Moon: More rocks!

Homer: The wilder and angrier you become, the more determined I'll be to overcome your obstacles.

> Homer gathers his strength and bursts into the sky, flying very swiftly.

Moon (laughing): The higher you fly, the closer you get to me.

Homer: You're already setting. I'm heading toward the sunrise.

Moon: I'm big and strong. I can cover the sun and make it dark here on the earth.

Homer: Please don't do that.

Moon: How can I prove to you that I have power?

Homer: Be nice to me.

Moon (laughing ironically): Hah! You want the whole universe to do your bidding. Forget it! I won't let you go any farther.

Homer (begging): Please don't tire me more than I am now.

Moon: I know you're tired. Why don't you stop and rest with me? I'm the nearest heavenly body.

Homer: I don't want to waste any more time. The sun will be rising soon.

> A bright ray of light from the planet Venus suddenly bursts from the dark sky and focuses on Homer. Moon's rays twist into the shape of an umbrella to shield Homer from the bright light.

Moon: Come quickly. Follow me before you become blind. There are many planets out there looking for someone like you to start a colony on them, but they can't sustain life. I'm the only heavenly body that fits your needs after the earth dries up. Come! Hurry! You are in danger.

Homer (screaming): I can't see anything. Turn that light off! Where is it coming from?

> Homer escapes from Venus' light and attempts to shield his eyes. Moon continues to shield Homer.

Moon (to Homer): Come. Hurry. Follow me.

Homer: What for? I already told you I'm heading toward the sun.

Moon: I want to protect you.

> Moon and Venus struggle, each using its rays like a sword. With the rays concentrating on each other, Homer escapes in the dark and flies higher.

Homer (to Moon): My eyes still hurt me, but at least I can see now.

> The light from Venus dominates the light of Moon.

Venus (to Moon): Get out of my way.

Moon: You can't have him.

Venus: Why not?

> Venus twists into a bright yellow ray, then bursts into the sky in pursuit of Homer.

Moon: I'm Homer's neighbour. I was the first heavenly body to offer a place to rest.

Venus: I'm the brightest star in the sky. I'm almost the size of the earth. I've been waiting for millions of years for someone to come to me. I think the day has come to take a living creature to live with me.

> The light from Venus covers Homer and turns him yellow. Moon pursues Homer with feeble gray rays.

Homer (to Moon): Where's this yellow light coming from? It's still beating down on me.

Venus (to Homer): I'm Venus! The brightest planet in the sky. (Loud laughter.) Follow my warm, colourful light, and I'll lead you to my hidden treasure, and if you are truly brave, you will discover my secrets.

Homer: I will not follow you. I have a goal. I cannot lose sight of it.

Venus: You have a goal?

Homer: Yes.

Venus: You could reach your goal if you follow me.

Homer: It's impossible to follow you.

Venus: If you were to live with me, everything would become possible.

Moon (to Venus): Nothing would be possible with you. I'm the only place where everything is possible; and it's up to Homer to bring me to life.

Venus (laughing ironically): If you're so good, why have you been lifeless for so long?

Moon: I've been waiting for Homer.

Venus: You can remain waiting then. Do you know why? I'll tell you why: because you are airless, waterless, and lifeless. Homer has no interest in you anymore.

Moon (angrily): How dare you talk about me like that! (To Homer.) Tell Venus how useful I am and why I've waited so long.

Homer (to Moon): I don't know. Maybe when I have achieved my dream, I'll think of you.

Venus (to Homer): Moon is hostile to life. It's pointless to think about it.

Moon (to Venus): I've at least had someone set foot on my soil.

Venus (tauntingly): Did they find any signs of life? You are a worthless piece of space junk. Do you know why anyone ever set foot on you in the first place?

Moon: Because I'm such a peaceful, serene heavenly body.

Venus (laughing): You are devoid of any life-forms. The only reason anyone landed on you in the first place is that you are close to earth. They had no way of reaching me then. I'm too far away.

Homer (angrily): I'm not interested in either of you. I'm flying to the sun. I'll use all my energy to achieve my dream. I'm the most powerful creature in this universe.

> Homer closes his eyes, flaps his wings three times, and flies away. Moon and Venus gather their rays into separate balls of light and give chase.

Venus: I want him.

Moon: No! He's mine.

Homer (joyfully): I'm faster.

> Homer continues to fly on his way, oblivious to the fighting between Moon and Venus. A ray of light from Mercury penetrates the darkness from the west and floods Homer.

Mercury (speaking very quickly): You can't run away from me. I am Mercury, the fastest body in the universe! I'm the friend of Mars and Venus. We are the closest stars to the earth. I invite you to stop and visit with me.

Homer (desperately): Here we go again! … I don't want any one of you. Why don't you all just leave me alone?

Mercury: My understanding is that you are not able to reach me because I am too far away; but I'm always ready to receive visitors because I believe in you. You can create heaven on my surface.

Homer: I don't want to.

Mercury: Don't be too hasty! I can harm you if you ignore me.

Homer concentrates on his flying. He pays no attention to Mercury.

Homer (to himself): I wish the sun would rise now!

Mercury (angrily): Are you ignoring me? I warned you! You will never see the sun!

Homer (triumphantly): They told me before that I couldn't fly. But look at me now! I'm high and I'm going to fly higher. The sun is so much on my mind that I can almost see an end to my dream.

Mercury: We stars will hide the sun from your sight.

Homer (laughing): You can't do that! The sun is the biggest star in the universe. It's the most important star to all living things. The sun gives us all life.

Mercury: I wish you would make me full of life, just like your planet, Earth.

Homer: You simply don't understand it, do you?

Mercury: What don't I understand?

Homer (slowly, with emphasis on each word): I – cannot – give – up – my – dream.

Mercury: But your dream is not realistic.

Homer: I have the capability to make it become real.

Mercury: How?

Homer: By working hard and by using my physical and intellectual abilities.

Mercury (angrily): You are a selfish being. You look only for an easy way to accomplish your dream.

Suddenly a ray of red light comes from the southeast. Homer tries to avoid it.

Homer (frightened): What is this? I'm scared!

The red light intensifies and soon dominates the scene. All is bathed in red.

Mercury (laughing): You see? I told you we could hide the sun. (Introducing Mars.) Homer, meet the planet Mars.

Mars draws a circle of light around Homer. Mercury's light hovers above Homer.

Mars (to Mercury): I've been waiting a long time to meet an earthly creature.

Mercury: Forget it. He's heading towards the sun.

Mars (firmly): We simply won't allow him to fly any farther.

Homer (to Mars): Would you please shut down your red light?

Mars: Oh, I can't do that! My light is on all the time. I survive on the sun's light.

Homer: I need the sun more than you do. I want to be as bright as the sun. That's why I'm heading there.

Mars: You will not reach it.

Homer: I've been told that before; but look at me now! I'm closer to the stars than I've ever been!

Mars: You are not. You only see our lights and hear our voices. You will be close to us only when you decide to live on one of us.

Homer: You are only stars, like the rest of the heavenly bodies.

Mars: I want you to put life on me, just as you have done on Earth. Do you know what happened to me a long, long time ago?

Homer: I'm not interested in what happened to you a long, long time ago!

Mercury (to Mars): Aha! He's interested in **me**!

Mars: **I'm** closer to him than **you** are.

Mercury: But he's going to the sun, and I am the closest star to the sun, so there!

Homer (to Mercury): Please, Mercury, can you help me?

Mercury: I'm sorry, I can't.

Homer (begging): I just want to rest on you for awhile until the sun rises.

Mercury: You said you were a powerful creature. Why are you asking for help?

Homer: Everyone needs help some time. To help someone is … to learn something.

Mercury: If you promise to stay with me from now on, I'll help you create a good life.

Mars (interrupting): Listen, Homer! Don't go too far away. Stay with me. I have everything you need.

> Homer is confused by all the lights. He attempts to escape to the darkness but Mars pursues him.

Homer: Get away — your light is too hot.

Mars: If you think I'm hot, how can you go to the sun? The sun is much hotter than I am.

Homer: Why are you hot like that?

Mars: It's only the sun's reflection. It'll be rising soon. I sure hope you can bring life to my lifeless soil.

Mercury (to Mars): You don't deserve to have any life-forms living on you.

Mars (to Mercury): Oh? And I suppose you do!

Mercury: Well, most certainly I do.

Mars: And why is that?

Mercury: Because I'm closest to the sun.

Mars: I once sustained life- forms many years ago.

Mercury: Prove it, then! When did life ever exist on Mars?

Mars: Homer will prove that life existed on me once upon a time.

> The lights of Mars and Mercury begin to fight with each other. Homer flies between them. Far from the northeast, the light of Venus enters the fray. The three engage in battle, while Homer escapes in the dark.

Venus (firmly): You both know that I have an atmosphere. I deserve to have Homer live with me.

Mars: I had life-forms once. Now I want them back.

Venus (laughing ironically): That was millions of years ago. You're hostile to life now, just like Moon.

Mars: I'm different from Moon.

Venus: In what ways are you different from Moon?

Mars: In every way!

Mercury: We shouldn't be arguing among ourselves. We should be convincing Homer that we can sustain life.

Mars: Where is he?

Homer is high above with just his feathers reflecting the faraway lights of Mars, Mercury, and Venus.

Venus: I must get to him before the sun rises.

Mercury: I'm faster. I'll get him.

The three lights gather themselves into balls and fly into the sky pursuing Homer. They form three colourful rings around Homer. Suddenly Moon sends its ray of gray light from the east and twists inside the rings, starting a battle with the yellow, red, and orange light rays.

Moon (firmly): You know I was the first heavenly body to have Homer. I will be next to be colonized.

Mars: I'm the planet of the next century. I'm nearest to the earth.

Moon: I may be alone and serene, but I will fight if necessary to secure my future.

Mars: Let Homer decide which heavenly body he wants to land on.

Venus: First, we have to stop him from flying so high. He will burn himself in the heat of the sun and then we'll lose him forever.

The light of Venus, Mars, and Mercury go on fighting and twisting into the depths of the sky. The sun's rays are seen beyond the horizon, slowly brightening up the sky. Moon pursues Homer in a feeble light. Soon all lights disappear as the sun's rays become stronger. Dawn has broken. Homer's voice is heard echoing all over the sky.

Homer's voice (singing):
Will the darkness last forever?
Will the stars be here to stay?
Will the night be long and dark?
Will the stars be in my way?
My dream will keep me flying 'til …

Scene Two

Dawn arrives. The darkness slowly gives way to light as the sky becomes bright. The stars disappear from the sky one by one. Homer is flying and singing joyfully.

Homer (singing):
The darkness comes to an end, the stars no longer shine.
The night turns into day, and the morning is sublime.
I'm flying to the sun ...

> The sky has become very bright now. The stars have completely disappeared. The Moon moves quickly toward the east, as its light also fades.

Homer (with excitement): Oh boy! It's daybreak! I made it!

Venus (appearing in the eastern sky, and sending a yellow beam of light towards Homer): You will never make it to the sun anyway.

Homer (proudly): I'm still flying! It means I'm going to meet the sun just over those hills.

Venus (laughing ironically): You are just dreaming about something far away.

Homer: I'm not just dreaming. I'm working very hard to achieve that dream.

Venus: What if you can't reach the sun? What will you do then, huh? Will you go back home or will you stop and live here with me?

Homer (ignoring Venus' comments): I can feel the warmth of the sun. I can see its rays.

He flies towards the rays of the sun, which can be seen just beyond the hills illuminating the sky in a halo of bright colours.

Venus (desperately): Just remember, my dear Homer, there may come a day when our presence in this universe will be just another one of your dreams; but I will not lose hope in you. I will wait until you come to the realization that we planets may some day sustain life again.

Homer (totally ignoring Venus): I'm going to the sun. I'll make my life as bright as the sun's light forever.

Venus: I wish you luck.

Venus disappears as the sun bursts into the sky above the hills in a ball of fire.

Homer (gazing at the sunrise in awe): Look at that! The king of stars! A gentle ball of fire, burning itself to light the others.

The Moon has almost set, and is seen as a silver ball with almost no reflection, its weak light barely visible on Homer.

Moon (to Homer): I'll show you how to make the King of Stars disappear from the sky!

Homer (laughing): Hah! You can't do anything to the sun! It's the most powerful body in the universe.

Moon (angrily): That just shows how little you know! Your knowledge of the universe is very limited. You really don't know about the powers in the heavenly bodies, do you?

Homer: You're not as bright as the sun. Look! It's moving toward you at a high speed!

Moon: I'll show you I'm big enough to cover the sun from your sight and make the landscape dark.

Homer: You can't cover the sun. (Moon moves toward the sun. The level of light diminishes noticeably. Homer flies up excitedly.) Why are you rushing toward the sun?

Moon (firmly): To show you my power and that I'm able to destroy your dream.

Homer (in a panic): No! Don't do that to me. Stop it! Stop it! Please stop! PLEASE!

> Moon's shadow continues relentlessly toward the sun.

Moon: Nothing can stop me from doing what is natural in this universe.

Homer (screaming): Don't destroy my big dream. Please go back.

> Moon reaches toward the sun, and slowly the sky becomes darker and darker until Moon covers the sun. A brilliant diamond ring appears around the Moon. A thin portion of the solar disc remains uncovered. The landscape darkens. Venus appears in the northeast sky, dropping its light onto Homer.

Venus (to Homer): I can't help you, Homer. It's the law of the universe. It's called the eclipse. It occurs when the sun, moon, and earth are precisely lined up in a certain way.

Homer: What can I do?

Venus: You'll have to figure it out for yourself. You are Homer.

Homer: I will never give up my dream. (He stops and thinks to himself.) Yes, I'm Homer.

> He stares at the sky thoughtfully, then looks down towards the darkened landscape. He gathers his wings to his body and aims down toward the ground. Moon has completely covered the sun. Only a bright circle is seen around Moon's dark silhouette.

ACT TWO
Scene One

Due to the eclipse, everything in Barnyardia is in darkness. The Moon completely covers the sun; the brilliant diamond ring around the moon shimmers. King Mortimer is in the castle yard, looking at the sky through his telescope. Mathilda, sitting beside him, looks nervously at the sky. Bartholomew, Prunella, Jeremiah, and Penelope are on the tree trunk looking at the sky in wide-eyed amazement. Sylvester is curled up snugly in a corner off to one side.

Jeremiah (surprised because of the dark): What's going on? Is it nighttime already? I can't believe it! The sun rose only a short time ago! It can't be bedtime yet. I'm not going to bed. I just woke up!

Bartholomew (to Jeremiah): I feel the cold has gone straight to my bones.

Prunella (to Penelope): Something has happened to the sun? That's it, isn't it?

Penelope (in amazement): I don't know what it is, but I can barely keep my eyes open!

Mathilda (also surprised): The sun has disappeared! Where is my little one?

King Mortimer (loudly): Don't look at the sun with your naked eyes. Where is Sylvester?

Sylvester quickly jumps from his bed.

Sylvester: Yes, my lord! I was sleeping. It's still night.

King Mortimer: It isn't night, it's only an eclipse. The moon has covered the sun for a moment. Go bring the special glasses that I prepared, and give them to everybody so we can watch the eclipse.

Sylvester (worrying): I wonder what happened to Homer?

King Mortimer (firmly): Don't worry about Homer. Bring the special glasses.

Sylvester: What for? My lord?

King Mortimer: To look at the sun. It's dangerous to look at it without special precautions. You may become blind. These glasses are specially fitted with a strong filter so we can look at the sun without hurting our eyes. Go get them!

Sylvester: What will happen to Homer? He has no special glasses.

King Mortimer: I told you before! Don't worry about Homer. He's smart enough to deal with the eclipse. Now go get the glasses! Hurry!

> Curiosity gets the better of Sylvester, and he takes a peek at the sun. He yelps and quickly covers his eyes with his hands.

King Mortimer (to Sylvester): You stubborn cat! I told you not to look directly at the sun!

Sylvester (screaming): Oh! Oh! My eyes! I feel as if they have been stabbed with a needle.

> He quickly goes away, covering his eyes with his hands.

King Mortimer: I can't imagine what has happened to Homer.

Mathilda (nervously): What's happened to my son? Can you see him?

King Mortimer: No, I can't. I don't know what's happened to him! He's nowhere in sight.

Mathilda: Do you think something horrible could have happened to him?

King Mortimer: Nothing's happened to him. I'm sure he's all right.

> Sylvester comes back carrying a box of glasses and hands them around, keeping a pair for himself.

Sylvester (to King Mortimer): Everyone has a pair of glasses, my King!

King Mortimer: Put them on. The sun will be reappearing soon.

Mathilda: What's that? Did you say my son will be reappearing soon?

King Mortimer: I believe your son will be back soon. I know he's smart enough to figure out what happened to the sun. (He turns to Sylvester.) Now put on the glasses, you silly oaf, or you will become blind.

> Sylvester pretends to put the glasses on, then takes them off.

Sylvester: I don't need special glasses … Okay. I'll put them on, but I don't really need them. I have good eyesight; I can see in the dark.

> They all look at the sun through their glasses except Sylvester. The sun emerges from behind the moon, and the landscape becomes brighter. The moon fades from the sky. All are looking intently at the sky. At this moment Homer appears, flying at a low level. He lands quietly.

Homer (to himself): What are they looking at? Hey, they're looking at the sun! (He whispers to Sylvester.) Sylvester. Sylvester.

> Sylvester turns towards the voice.

Sylvester: Who's calling me? I can't see! (He wipes his eyes.) What's happened to my eyes?

Homer (whispering): It's me! Homer!

Sylvester: Homer? Is it really you? (He turns first in one direction, then another.) Where are you? Homer! (He addresses the rest of the group.) Hey, guys! He's back. Homer's back! And he's alive! Homer, where are you? I can't see you! What's wrong? I can't see! I'm blind! Homer, help me! Please!

They all turn toward Homer and take off their glasses.

All together (loudly): Homer … alive!

Mathilda runs to Homer and hugs him tightly.

Mathilda: My son! You're back! We missed you terribly! (scolding) I hope you realize that it was only a foolish dream to fly to the sun. You don't know how terrified I was that I might never see you again. (soothingly) Let's go back to Lake Serenity.

Homer (hugging his mother): I missed you very much, too, Mother; but I'm not going back. I learned a lot while I was away, and I now want to discover whether there is life on the stars.

Mathilda: There you go again! Another big dream?

They all laugh at him except Sylvester, who is still wiping his eyes and trying to open them.

Sylvester: My eyes! Where are all of you? I can't see anything.

All look at him silently for a moment. King Mortimer approaches Sylvester and examines his eyes.

King Mortimer (sadly): Sylvester! (He shakes his head.) Oh! Sylvester, my faithful servant and excellent chef, and oh-so-foolish cat! What have you done? (He turns to Homer.) You see what comes of foolishness and being hardheaded. (He turns back to Sylvester.) I told you not to look directly at the sun!

Sylvester (sobbing): Do you mean I've lost my sight forever?

King Mortimer: That's what I think.

Sylvester (crying loudly): My lord! What can I do now?

> Sylvester sobs pitifully. All surround him and look at him sympathetically.

King Mortimer (to Sylvester): You are now just a worthless cat. I don't need you here in my kingdom. I don't need a blind servant, and a blind chef cannot perform his duties properly.

> All turn to King Mortimer, gasping. They stand and stare at him in disbelief.

Sylvester (sadly): But I have no place to go. How can you exile me from the kingdom after so many years of serving you so faithfully? Have you no compassion?

> Homer gives a warm hug to Sylvester, then approaches King Mortimer politely.

Homer: My King, I need your help. Would you help me, please?

King Mortimer (angrily): I have always helped anyone who lived peacefully in this kingdom and abided by our rules. (He turns to Sylvester.) But you, Sylvester, you chose not to listen to my warning about looking at the sun. Now look at you! Who wants a blind chef? (He turns accusingly to Homer.) These troubles are all your fault. You and your silly dream of flying to the sun!

Homer (softly to the king): Please don't turn me down. You are a kind and generous king.

King Mortimer (angrily): It's time for you to go home.

Homer (begging): Please! Help me just this once, and I'll never bother you again.

King Mortimer: I have no magic powers. I can't help you fly again. If I had any magic I would bring Sylvester's sight back.

Homer: My King! I only want your telescope.

King Mortimer (with surprise): What?

Homer (shyly): I want to look at the sun. ... (He hesitates.) ... No, I want to look at the stars.

King Mortimer: My telescope is my most prized possession! (He holds the telescope tenderly.) I cannot give it to just anyone!

Homer (insisting): I only want to look at the stars and study them.

King Mortimer (angrily to Mathilda): Would you please take your troublemaking son back to Lake Serenity, and leave us alone?

Mathilda (defiantly): My son is not a troublemaker.

King Mortimer (calmly): I didn't mean to anger you. I want you to leave before the widow Lucy Goose and that troublemaker Henrietta Chicken come back. You will be in big trouble if they see your son here again.

Mathilda: At least my son knows how to fly!

King Mortimer: And that should be enough for him. Now, take him and go home.

Mathilda (to Homer): Let's go.

Homer: I can't leave Sylvester by himself like that. He's my friend.

King Mortimer (in a loud peremptory voice): I have ordered you to leave! Now!

Homer (pleading): Please, King Mortimer, I beg your pardon. I did not mean to anger you.

King Mortimer: I don't want any more trouble because of you. Now leave us alone!

Homer: I have become one of your family.

King Mortimer: We don't need you. We have enough in our family right now.

Homer: I can take care of you and Sylvester, too.

> King Mortimer laughs and hops from branch to branch, looking in all directions before coming to Homer.

King Mortimer: You? Homer? Looking after me? You destroyed my peaceful life. (He again pleads with Mathilda.) Please take your son away. I don't want to see him here any longer.

> He turns and stalks away. Mathilda approaches Homer and tries to take him by the hand.

Homer: Mother! Don't kill my dream.

Mathilda: I won't. But the king doesn't want to see you here. It's better for us to leave. We have a nice place at Lake Serenity. You can pursue your dream there.

Homer (thoughtfully): Mother, you don't understand! I already started my dream. I must continue. (He pauses.) Mother! Not long ago you told me that if I had a dream, I should work hard to achieve it.

Mathilda (nodding her head): Yes, that's right, Son. (She prepares to leave.) We should be going back now, Homer. I can't live away from the lake for very long.

Homer: I know, Mother, you like our lake. You will always be with me. You are in my heart, Mother! But I just have to do what I feel is right for me.

Mathilda (tearfully): I love you so much, Son.

Homer: I love you, too, Mother!

They hug each other tightly for a moment. Then suddenly Mathilda breaks away from Homer, sobbing, and runs away into the forest.

Mathilda's voice: I love you, Son!

Homer pursues her to the edge of the forest.

Homer (tearfully): See you soon, Mother. Good-bye!

Homer comes back to the telescope, looks at the sky, and then sits near the telescope thoughtfully.

Scene Two

It is midday. The sun shines brightly. The broken down tree is on the ground. Sylvester sits on the ground beside the tree trunk feeling miserable. Homer sits near the telescope, deep in thought. Penelope and Jeremiah have started cleaning up the mess. Bartholomew and Prunella are pushing away a big branch. King Mortimer enters. He seems restless and nervous.

King Mortimer (looking at the sun): The Queen will be back soon. (He sees Homer.) Are you still here?

Homer: Why do you want me to leave, my King?

King Mortimer: I want you to leave so the young generation can rebuild this kingdom.

> He gestures towards Penelope and Jeremiah in a sweeping motion with his arm.

Homer: You're right, my lord: we, the new generation, will build a new future together.

King Mortimer: There can be no future for the new generation if the kingdom is in turmoil.

Homer (gestures to the sky): There's a whole new kingdom out there. We can explore new worlds.

King Mortimer (angrily): You're just dreaming! Leave now. (He looks at the sun.) It's almost time. I don't want another fight because of you. (He turns to Penelope.) I'm putting you in charge. Take care of the kingdom and get everything ready for the Queen.

Sylvester gets up and walks towards Penelope to help her. He bangs his head into a low branch.

Sylvester (rubbing his forehead): Ouch! My forehead! I want to meet the Queen. I want to serve the Queen. (He trips on a loose branch and falls down.) Help me! ... I want my sight back.

Homer goes to Sylvester and helps him get up.

Homer: Just be patient. It's not the end of the universe. We can still make a difference.

Sylvester (whining): I want my sight back!

King Mortimer (to Homer): If you think you can make a difference, then give Sylvester's sight back.

Homer (sadly): If only I could!

King Mortimer: You could ... if you weren't such a daydreamer — if you dreamed about realistic goals instead of those fanciful unachievable ones of yours! (He addresses Penelope and Jeremiah.) Go get Homer and bring him to me. (He then addresses Prunella and Bartholomew.) You, bring the wire and tie him to the tree trunk and let him stay all day facing the sun. Maybe then he'll realize that his dream is a foolish one and impossible to achieve. (He shouts.) Go! Do as I say! Now!

Penelope and Jeremiah stand transfixed, looking at Homer. They cannot believe their ears.

King Mortimer: What are you waiting for? (He takes a step towards Penelope.) Move! You are in charge of the kingdom. From now on you are the chief cook. (Nobody moves.) We have to get rid of this homeless duck. (He points to Homer.) Bring him to me, I said!

All remain silent, unmoving, looking at Homer.

Homer (murmuring to Sylvester): The King has lost control — of himself — and the kingdom.

Sylvester: What do you mean?

Homer: I think it's time for us to take charge and start to build our future together.

King Mortimer takes a few steps towards Sylvester, then goes back to Penelope furiously.

King Mortimer: You young people have forgotten your duties and ignore the rules of this kingdom. (He steps towards Homer.) You have ruined our life! You with your stubborn refusal to see what's right, insisting on having your own way, instead of listening to your wiser elders! (He whirls about, facing the crowd which has now encircled him.) Why are all of you looking at Homer with such admiration? Can't you see what he's doing? He'll ruin all of us — and the kingdom, too! Seize him! He must be stopped! Bring him to me!

They all remain in their places, looking at Homer.

Homer (whispering to Sylvester): I think this is the end. The King no longer has the respect of the citizens of Barnyardia. He's finished as leader. Nobody will listen to him.

King Mortimer (looking up at the sun): Where is the Queen? It's almost lunchtime. She should be here by now. (He turns to Penelope.) Go get the red carpet. (He gives an order to Prunella.) You go set the table. (He looks at Sylvester.) Where is the food? What will the Queen eat? (Sadly.) Oh! My poor Sylvester! Who will feed us?

Homer: My lord! Don't worry about the food.

King Mortimer: But food is everything to us. If we don't eat regularly, we can't survive. Why are you looking at me like that? Am I a stranger in this kingdom? (He stands defiantly and shouts.) I am King Mortimer, King of Barnyardia! Everyone must do his duty. Get a move on! Go!

All remain in their places, looking at him silently.

King Mortimer: What do you want me to do? (He pushes Penelope.) Move! Do something! (He pauses. When nobody moves at his command, he loses some of his bluster. He is perplexed. He takes a step in one direction, then another. Realizing that nobody is obeying, he acquiesces.) I see! You want me to do everything myself. Well I don't mind doing everything for my wife. I'll get the red carpet myself. She deserves to walk on a red carpet. (He goes off for the carpet.)

Homer (to Sylvester): See? I told you. It's time to take over.

Sylvester: What about me? How will I survive?

Homer: I'll look after you. We can live and work together.

Sylvester: What about my eyes?

Homer: Don't worry, my friend. My eyes are yours. I will tell you everything that happens in our life. We will share our dream.

> Everyone surrounds Homer and looks at him with admiration. Just then King Mortimer comes back carrying a red carpet.

King Mortimer (breathing heavily from the exertion): Where is the Queen?

> He sets the red carpet down. Nigel and Priscilla Pigeon fly into the area. Homer sees them.

Homer (to Sylvester): Oh! Sylvester, look! Your friends are here. (To Nigel and Priscilla.) Thank goodness you're safe.

> They land on a branch not far away from Sylvester.

Priscilla: We have a message for the King.

Sylvester (sadly to himself): If my sight ever comes back to me, I will never harm anyone.

> King Mortimer is rolling out the red carpet, anxiously looking towards the forest periodically.

King Mortimer (to Priscilla): Where is the Queen? What kind of message do you have?

Priscilla: The Queen sent us to tell you that she, Henrietta Chicken, and Lucy Goose are not coming back from Lake Serenity. They want all of you to move down there with them, close to the lake.

King Mortimer (confused): What? What lake?

Nigel: Lake Serenity, of course. Homer's lake.

King Mortimer: What about our kingdom?

Homer: We'll take good care of it.

King Mortimer: How can the Queen give up her kingdom? She must have seen something awfully tempting to convince her not to return here! I must go to see her. I can't live without her.

> King Mortimer prepares to leave. Homer stops him.

Homer: Please, my lord, wait a minute.

> King Mortimer stops. Homer quickly lines up Penelope, Jeremiah, Bartholomew, and Prunella in two lines facing each other, then guides Sylvester to the end of the carpet to say farewell to King Mortimer.

King Mortimer: I spent all my youth in this kingdom! I dreamed of being king one day! I achieved my dream. Now I am king! How can I give up my kingdom?

Homer (calmly): My lord! You are not giving up your kingdom. You are only doing what is natural. We, the new generation, want to achieve our dream, too.

King Mortimer (tearfully): Do you mean my time is over?

Homer (thinking): Every era has its time. Good-bye, my lord. We wish you the happiest time for the rest of your life.

> King Mortimer steps onto the red carpet very slowly. Homer gives a signal to start singing.

All together (singing):
Saying good-bye doesn't mean good-bye forever.
Saying good-bye means for just a little while.
From time to time we'll meet again; so until then,
Good-bye to you from us. Good-bye to us from you.

> King Mortimer walks slowly to the edge of the forest. He stops, glances at them, they wave good-bye to him, and he disappears into the forest. The song echoes all over the forest.

End of Part III

Part Four

A New Beginning

Even though the sun seemed to disappear during the eclipse, and it seemed that the universe was against Homer, he did not give up on his dream to become an astronaut and fly to the sun. He learned how to overcome all obstacles. Now he's getting ready for the biggest part of his dream: he's going to fly in space! Maybe he'll visit the planet most likely to have life-forms on it — the Red Planet Mars! Does life exist elsewhere in the universe?

The answer is in the conclusion to Homer's dream in Part IV, "A New Beginning"!

The dream is realized...

In Part I, "A Duckling's Dream," we met Homer, an ambitious and determined young duckling. His one dream was to fly to the sun. He met and overcame many obstacles on his quest. With the support of his young friends, and the supernatural powers of the king of Barnyardia, Homer eventually realized the beginning of his dream — he could fly! As Part I ended, Homer was on his way, flying to the sun.

In Part II, "Against the Odds," Homer met even more formidable opponents. The elements of nature took exception to his exploits, and banded together to stop his foolhardiness. Homer took on the challenges of nature's powerful elements as he continued his journey to the sun. Who would be the ultimate victor in this titanic struggle? Was Nature powerful enough to stop a young duckling's dream? Or was determination and willpower enough to overcome all hardships? Homer eventually succeeded because he was determined to get what he had set his heart on. Despite the anger of the wild wind and the other elements, Homer was able to continue his journey.

In Part III, "Journey through Space," Homer had grown into a fine young drake, and continued his quest on a dark night full of bright stars. The stars, the Moon, and the planets Venus, Mercury, and Mars all wanted Homer to stay with them and discover what they had to offer. He refused their offers, and they became very angry. When the Moon hid the sun from his view, Homer began to have doubts as to whether he would ever achieve his dream. He returned home only to find that conditions had deteriorated to the point where someone had to take charge. He did just that, and as Part III ended, we were beginning to see a possible light at the end of this dark tunnel.

Part IV, "A New Beginning," is the conclusion to this odyssey. Homer has grown into adulthood. He and his childhood friends are adults, and are taking control of the kingdom of Barnyardia. They have constructed a new space centre on the site of the old castle, and are about to embark on a flight into space. No longer content just to fly, they now want to fly to Mars!

The Characters

Homer	a duckling, mission control commander
Sylvester	a blind cat, pilot of the spaceship Homer 1
Jeremiah	a cockerel, director of flight operations
Penelope	a pullet, assistant director of flight operations
Bartholomew	a male gosling, flight navigations officer
Prunella	a female gosling, communications coordinator
King Mortimer	a turkey tom, retired king of Barnyardia
Queen Hortense	a turkey hen, retired queen of Barnyardia
Lucy	a goose, mother of Prunella and Bartholomew
Henrietta	a hen, mother of Penelope and Jeremiah
Mathilda	a duck, Homer's mother
Nigel	a male pigeon
Priscilla	a female pigeon

The Setting

King Mortimer Space Centre

Prologue

Lake Serenity seems almost too peaceful. Its surface is absolutely still and reflects the sky perfectly. Birds fly above the water making chirping and singing sounds. It's springtime. The sky is clear. The setting sun seems to touch the edge of the water. King Mortimer sits on a branch with his feet touching the water; around him are Queen Hortense, Lucy Goose, and Henrietta Chicken. They look at the sunset with enjoyment. Nigel and Priscilla appear, flying towards King Mortimer. They land close to King Mortimer.

Nigel (excitedly): They've finished everything. They are ready to launch the rocket!

> Priscilla gets closer to King Mortimer and flaps her wings.

Priscilla: They built a huge aircraft and now they're going to send it into space!

> King Mortimer gazes at the sunset, paying no attention to Priscilla and Nigel.

Nigel (to Priscilla): He's not listening! He doesn't care!

Priscilla: We have to let them know about the rocket.

Nigel: Yes, we must! (He whispers to King Mortimer.) King Mortimer! They will launch Homer 1 soon. You have to watch the sky. (To Priscilla.) I don't know what their problem is! What are they looking at?

> The sun sets completely. The sky remains red; the water reflects the sunset. King Mortimer turns to Nigel.

King Mortimer: Nigel! You're back! What were you saying?

Nigel: Homer 1 will soon burst into the sky.

King Mortimer (surprised): What do you mean?

Priscilla (excitedly): They are going to fly to the planets.

King Mortimer: Who's going to fly? Where? To Mars?

Priscilla: I don't know which planet, but soon Homer 1 will be bursting into the sky.

King Mortimer: But you don't know which planet they're headed for?

Nigel: They studied the planets very carefully, especially the closest ones to the earth. (He is hardly able to control his excitement.) They are ready to launch the rocket!

> Lucy Goose and Henrietta Chicken move closer to Nigel. Queen Hortense watches the sky intently.

King Mortimer (to Nigel): Will they all fly?

Nigel: I don't think so. The spacecraft is big enough for only one pilot.

King Mortimer: Then who will fly it?

Nigel: I don't know.

King Mortimer: Well, who's the pilot? I mean, from which family will the flyer come? Will it be a Chicken, Goose, or Duck to be first to fly in the rocket?

> Henrietta Chicken and Lucy Goose eye each other warily, then begin to circle Nigel, hoping the answer will reveal one of their family as the lucky choice.

Nigel: I couldn't find out who would fly in the rocket. It seems they all are eligible. I could hardly believe it when I heard even Sylvester shouting, "I want to fly ... I want to fly!"

King Mortimer (with great surprise): Sylvester wants to fly? That's preposterous! Cats can't fly.

There is a moment of silence as they all look at one another.

Nigel: I don't know. Why not?

King Mortimer: How come Sylvester wants to fly? He's blind. He's lost his sight. How can he guide a spacecraft? It's impossible to send someone blind into space. I believe it will be a Goose or a Chicken that will have to fly. (He turns to Henrietta Chicken) ... One of the Chickens perhaps, or ... (turning to Lucy Goose) maybe a Goose; ... or maybe it'll be Homer Duck himself.

Nigel: Homer is the leader of the team at the space centre.

Lucy (to Nigel): What space centre are you talking about?

Nigel: I'm talking about the King Mortimer Space Centre.

Lucy: The King Mortimer Space Centre? I've never heard of it before!

They stare in disbelief at King Mortimer for a moment.

Nigel: The Castle of Barnyardia does not exist anymore. In its place they have built a space centre and named it the King Mortimer Space Centre.

King Mortimer (proudly): Do you mean it's named after me? I'll be remembered for generations! Me? King Mortimer, the one who helped Homer achieve his dream! How about that!

Lucy: Well I certainly don't want my children influenced by a silly duckling's dream.

Nigel: They are definitely going to launch the rocket. It will happen pretty soon.

Lucy: I won't have my children flying around in a risky rocket. Why doesn't Homer Duck fly by himself? He's the one who wants to fly all the time. I want my children to live here with me at Lake Serenity.

King Mortimer (to Lucy): That would be the worst thing you ever did in your life, if you were to force your children to live where they weren't happy.

Lucy: Why?

King Mortimer: It should be their choice whether they want to fly or not.

Lucy: But I don't want my children to fly.

King Mortimer: Why not? It's an honour to fly. It's an achievement of a lifetime.

Lucy (desperately): I want my children beside me.

King Mortimer: It's too late, my dear Lucy! It's been over a year since they started working as a team. If you try to bring your children here now, it would be a waste of time.

Lucy (tearfully): I didn't expect my children to fly to other planets. They are so young.

King Mortimer: We have to expect many things from the younger generation. It's their world.

 Henrietta Chicken gets closer to King Mortimer.

Henrietta (quietly): I never expected my children to fly any higher than the garbage barrel. (proudly) Now, I'm happy and proud to see their rocket ship go into deep space.

 Lucy Goose approaches Henrietta Chicken and pushes her away, then turns to King Mortimer.

Lucy (sarcastically): Of course Henrietta Chicken is proud of her sons!

They never **could** fly any higher than the garbage dump! (Gestures to Henrietta.) Now they want to visit other planets? (She laughs.) Hah! It's a dream! A silly duck's even sillier dream! I won't let my sons risk their lives on such a silly pipe dream.

Henrietta (to King Mortimer): It's not risky to fly, is it, my lord? Besides, I agree with our king when he said that we have to give freedom to the younger generation. My sons know what they're aiming for.

Lucy: I have to look after my sons until they're old enough to look after themselves.

King Mortimer (to Lucy): Your sons have already made their choice, I'm afraid, Lucy. It's their lives, and they are old enough to know what they want.

Lucy: How very awful for me. How could they choose the direction their lives will take without my agreement? (She pauses, then stamps her foot.) … I'm their mother! I have the right to tell them what's wrong and what's right. (She takes a deep breath.) My sons never behaved like that before. They always listened to me. I never expected a little duckling to influence my sons. It's all Homer's fault. How did his mother let him go and take such risks?

Henrietta: It's simple. She loves her son; therefore, she gave him his freedom.

Lucy (laughing ironically): Freedom has its boundaries. If we let the younger generation go beyond those boundaries, theirs will be a dangerous freedom.

> Mathilda Duck appears swimming toward the edge of the lake. King Mortimer sees her.

King Mortimer (calling): Mathilda! Mathilda Duck! Come over here. (He turns to Hortense.) She is very proud of Homer.

Queen Hortense: I'm proud of him, too.

King Mortimer: Me, too. I'm proud of our hero Homer. I will honour him with the highest award in Barnyardia.

> Mathilda Duck swims closer to King Mortimer. Lucy and Henrietta approach the edge of the water, angrily waiting for Mathilda Duck.

Lucy (to Henrietta): Look at her! She doesn't seem to care at all about what her son is doing. She gave up all her duties as a mother long ago.

> Mathilda Duck gets out of the water.

King Mortimer (to Mathilda): Your son, Homer, ...

Mathilda (interrupting with a worried expression on her face): What's happened to my son?

King Mortimer (continuing): ... is going to fly in a spaceship.

Mathilda: I will not let him fly anymore. He tried once. That's enough for him. I want him to be safe beside me here at the lake.

> Lucy Goose and Henrietta Chicken get closer to Mathilda Duck and try to push her back into the water.

Lucy: We don't need you. You're not fit to be a mother.

> Mathilda Duck brushes them out of the way and walks towards King Mortimer and Queen Hortense.

Mathilda: Where is my son?

King Mortimer: The Queen and I are proud of Homer. (He looks at the sky.) Soon we shall see the rocket bursting into the sky, on its way to the other planets. It's a dream come true.

Mathilda (with surprise): What do you mean? What rocket? What are you talking about?

King Mortimer: Have no fear! He'll make it. I believe in your son's dream. It was once my dream, too, to fly to other planets. I have been dreaming all my life about the possibility of life on other planets and for us to discover it. Now it looks as if we're finally going to do just that!

Mathilda: I don't want my son to live on another planet.

King Mortimer: Let him go.

Mathilda: No. I don't have anyone to take care of me except Homer.

King Mortimer: We will take care of each other. Let the new generation make their life the way they want it. (proudly) We, the citizens of Barnyardia, will soon have one of us on the Red Planet, or some other planet. (He turns to Mathilda Duck.) You're a good teacher and mother. You taught Homer courage. It's a good lesson. You are the perfect mother.

> Henrietta Chicken and Lucy Goose look at each other, then scream angrily.

Henrietta: I want my little one to fly, I want to be a perfect mother, too.

Lucy: I'm the perfect mother. I taught my sons to be courageous, too.

King Mortimer: We have to watch the sky. A citizen of Barnyardia is going to make it to the Red Planet.

> They all gaze upwards at the sky.

Henrietta: I want my family's name to be known on the other planets.

Lucy: Wait a minute. What about **my** family's name? I want **my** family's name known on the other planets.

King Mortimer (to the Queen): I'm glad I lived long enough to see one of us blast off to another planet. (He turns proudly to Mathilda Duck.) Your son is everyone's hero.

Mathilda (proudly): My son — a hero!

King Mortimer: That's what I said about Homer when I first saw him. He's our hero! (He looks upward at the sky.) Soon the journey will begin to the Red Planet … a part of my life's dream is coming true.

Lucy (to King Mortimer): You, too, dreamed that some day you would fly like Homer?

King Mortimer: Yes, I did. I didn't have the courage, then, that the new generation has today. I'm proud of Homer and his friends. Our planet will be the first in this universe to discover other civilizations before our life here on earth is endangered.

Lucy: My lord, why should our life be in danger?

King Mortimer: We, on this planet, have to protect ourselves. We're not alone in the universe. There will come a time when everyone on this planet will be united by a common bond. There'll be no difference between countries or continents. The differences will be between planets. Every planet in this universe will have to struggle to maintain its independence and very existence.

Lucy: When will this happen, my lord?

King Mortimer: I don't know, but I do know what we, on this planet, must do.

Lucy: And what is that?

King Mortimer: We must discover the secrets of the other planets, because the first planet that does so becomes the power in the universe. All the world will be grateful to Homer! (loudly) Homer will be the world's hero!

Lucy (screaming): I want **my** sons to fly! I want **them** to be world heroes.

Henrietta (screaming): I want the **Chickens** to be the most famous in the world.

Mathilda (jubilant): I am a **Duck**! I am the hero's mother! Mine is the most famous name. The **Ducks** are the swimmers and the fliers in this world!

King Mortimer sits. All sit around him.

King Mortimer (quietly): It's time for our planet to create a united front against any outsiders. (He beckons to Nigel and Priscilla Pigeon.) Go back and tell Homer that we're waiting to see the rocket burst into the sky towards the Red Planet.

Nigel and Priscilla flap their wings and fly away.

Mathilda (loudly): Priscilla! Tell Homer I love him very much.

King Mortimer gets up and looks at the sky and starts to sing.

King Mortimer (singing):
Let them fly;
Let them be high;
Let them burst into the sky.

All together (singing):
Let them fly;
Let them be high;
Let them burst into the sky.

King Mortimer (singing):
Our dreams are linked to their dreams.
We're the first who paved the path
For the new generation to think.
Let them go.
The universe is vast. …
Let them do what they can
To bring honour to their past.

All together (singing):
    Let them fly;
    Let them be high;
    Let them burst into the sky.

> The sound of the song echoes all over the lake for a long time, then slowly fades.

End of Prologue

ACT ONE
Scene One

Inside the Control Room of the King Mortimer Space Centre. Three corridors lead off the Control Room, one to the right, another to the left, and a third, wider and brighter than the others, in the centre. A large viewing screen faces the central corridor. Television monitors are at the front of the control room. On the large screen is a close-up of a rocket ship with the name "Homer 1" on it. Also visible is a symbol of an olive branch with seven leaves and seven olives, representative of the earth's seven continents.

It is morning on the first day of summer. The sky, visible on the viewing screen, is clear and blue. The sun is about to rise. Homer enters the Control Room from the central corridor. He is wearing a white jacket and black pants. On the left lapel of the jacket is the olive branch symbol with seven leaves and seven black olives. Jeremiah and Penelope enter from the right corridor wearing navy-blue uniforms. On the left lapels of their jackets is an olive branch with four leaves and four green olives. Bartholomew and Prunella enter from the left corridor wearing yellow uniforms. Their jacket lapels show an olive branch with four leaves and four black olives. They sit around a table facing the viewing screen. Homer, pacing the control room, is deep in thought. He stops and glances at the monitor for a moment.

Homer (sitting down): My dream to fly to the sun is over. It was just a foolish child's dream. (He laughs.) But this … (pointing to the rocket ship on the screen) … this is not a dream! This is real! This is Homer 1. We built the rocket! The question now is who will guide it to the Red Planet? … (He pauses.) … I don't want you to get bogged down thinking about who is the best pilot, or who deserves the honour, or who you should vote for. ... (Another pause.) ... I want every one of you to think about yourself and say, "I want to fly! Why shouldn't **I** be the one to guide our rocket ship?" ... (There is a long silence.) ... I will not force you to fly if you don't want to. There should be an inner satisfaction in doing something that you like to do and want to do. We have to launch this rocket on schedule. We cannot give up on this mission to the Red Planet. We are finally about to achieve what we've long dreamed of. We worked hard to build our dream, and everyone participated in this project. It is time now to take our next step. ... (He pauses again.) ... I have a suggestion.

> They all look at Homer in anticipation. Suddenly the sound of slamming doors comes from the central corridor. All turn toward the sound.

Sylvester's voice (loudly in the back of the corridor somewhere): I want to fly! I want to fly!

Homer (laughing): He's still shouting. Ever since yesterday! I don't know how to convince him that we cannot allow him to fly on this mission!

> The sound of crashing and slamming of doors continues.

Sylvester's voice (screaming): Oh, my head! I will not give up on my dream so easily. (The crashing gets closer and more intense.) Where is that blasted door?

Homer (to Penelope): Could you please give him a hand?

> Penelope quickly exits into the centre corridor, looking for Sylvester.

Sylvester's voice (loudly): I want to fly! Why won't you believe that I can do it? Where is Homer? (He shouts loudly.) I want to fly!

Homer: It's nice to see such optimism. I only hope that we can all have the same positive outlook in the face of adversity that Sylvester Cat has. He believes he can guide Homer 1 to the Red Planet even though he is blind. I applaud his courage. … (He pauses.) … But we must forget Sylvester and his eagerness to fly! We have a decision to make before midday. Who is going to take Homer 1 up into space? Each one of us has the necessary skills to fly, but which one of us has the necessary courage?

Penelope enters guiding Sylvester.

Sylvester (eagerly): I can do it! I know I can! Just allow me to fly, please! Homer! Where are you? (He turns around in a circle, facing one way then another, trying to find Homer.) I am a good space pilot. I want to fly. I can complete the Homer 1 mission. Don't be fooled by my poor eyesight. I can still think, and I have other superior abilities. I want to be part of this historic mission.

Homer: My dear Sylvester, we need someone who has good vision. That doesn't mean we don't need you anymore. You gave us many ideas during the building process of the centre; but the crew of Homer 1 must be in good physical condition. And that means good vision, too.

Sylvester: You think I'm handicapped because I can't see? What about my other abilities?

Homer: We have no doubt about your courage and ambition. Nor do we doubt your intellectual abilities, but our mission is not just an adventure to the planets. We want to put everything in its proper place. We can't take chances.

Sylvester: Who will fly the ship, then?

Homer (thinking): Maybe I will.

They look at Homer silently. Sylvester turns around.

Sylvester: Why are the Chickens and Geese silent? Don't any of you want to fly in space? What's the matter? Don't you have the courage? (He pauses as he waits for a response.) . . . You see? None of them are interested. But **I** want to fly! I'm not afraid. I WANT TO FLY!

Homer (calmly): I believe it's a difficult decision for everyone. This is a dangerous mission.

Sylvester: You have to let me fly to the other planets to fulfill my dream.

Homer gazes at the monitor for a moment thoughtfully.

Homer: I'm not eager to let Sylvester fly. It's too risky for him and for the mission.

Sylvester (angrily): I may have lost my vision, but I haven't lost all my senses. I can tell what every one of you is thinking about me. (He points to Homer.) You're the team leader and my friend; yet you think that I am incapable of doing a good job on this mission. Do you really think that I have nothing to contribute to this team? (Loudly.) I want to fly!

Homer (gently): My dear Sylvester, if you only knew how much I care about you and how I want our mission to the Red Planet to be successful. . . .

Sylvester: I will do everything to make your dream come true. I remember the first day you came to Barnyardia. You told me that you wanted to fly and touch the edge of the sun. I laughed at you then. Now I think I know what you meant about touching the edge of the sun. You really want to fly in space. Well, so do I! **I want to fly.**

Homer: But we need someone with your talents here at the space centre.

Sylvester: And just what would I be doing here?

Homer: A very important function. You would be coordinating the flight. Besides, I told you before, my eyes are yours. I will tell you everything about the journey from the day Homer 1 is launched until the day it returns.

Sylvester (furiously): What do you take me for, my dear Homer! I want to be like everyone else at the space centre. I don't want special treatment.

Homer: Just calm down. You have greatly inspired us with all your tremendous ideas. You are a full participating member in the King Mortimer Space Centre, but we just cannot allow you to fly. I'm personally against allowing you to fly the spacecraft. (He turns to Penelope and Prunella.) What about you Chickens and Geese? Do you agree with me?

All four nod their heads in agreement.

Sylvester: They are all against me, too?

Homer: Yes, they don't want you to fly.

Sylvester (sadly): Because I'm blind?

Homer: Not because you are blind. We all want our mission to be a success.

Sylvester: You don't have confidence in me. Am I right?

They look at him with sympathy.

Homer: My dear Sylvester …

Sylvester (interrupting him): Don't say anything more. The most important thing to me is that I have confidence in myself. I know I can pilot Homer 1 to the Red Planet or to any other planet in the universe, for that matter.

Homer: No doubt you can. We know you have the skills, but we have to be ready for all circumstances. We have to be sure about everything.

And for that eventuality, our pilot must have complete control over all his senses in case suddenly he has to make a split-second decision in an emergency. (He pauses.) ... We feel sorry for you, my dear Sylvester, but we just cannot take the chance on something as important as this.

Sylvester (angrily): I don't want you or anybody else to feel sorry for me.

> He turns and takes a step towards the control table. He doesn't see a small stool and trips on it, falling down onto the control panel. Everything lights up. The alarm sounds and the emergency lights go on.

Homer: What happened?

> Everyone attempts to figure out what happened. Sylvester falls onto the floor. The control room starts shaking. There is a close-up of the rocket on the monitor. Thick smoke starts coming from the rocket. They all look at the monitor.

Penelope: The rocket's engines have been activated!

Sylvester (loudly): I want to fly! I want to fly!

Homer: Who touched the launch button?

> Homer quickly jumps to the control table and studies the switches briefly. He presses buttons and pulls switches, frantically attempting to stop the launch.

Sylvester (questioning): Do you mean to say you've launched the rocket without a pilot?

Homer (sighing with relief): Whew! Almost lost everything there because of a single small mistake.

> The lights of the control table turn off. The rocket on the

monitor stops spewing smoke. The sound of the alarm shuts down. They all sit quietly.

Sylvester: What happened?

They all look at him silently.

Homer: Don't you know? You almost destroyed the entire mission with that one small stumble. Now do you see why we can't let you fly?

Sylvester walks towards the control table searching with his hands.

Homer (shouting): Not that way! Get away from the control table.

Sylvester stops and moves again towards the control table.

Sylvester: Which way do you want me to go?

Homer: Just don't move. Don't do anything.

Sylvester: Do you mean it was my mistake?

Homer: You have to be careful. Just listen to us — don't touch any buttons!

Sylvester leans on the wall sadly.

Sylvester: I see. I'm in the way. You don't need me anymore.

Homer: We don't need your mistakes, Sylvester. You can't fly. (He looks at the wall clock.) We're wasting time. We have to decide who will go into space. Sit down.

They all sit around the table except Sylvester.

Penelope (to Homer): You're the one who always wanted to fly. Why not you now?

Homer (thinking): We are a team and everybody has a responsibility. Mine is to control the mission from the space centre.

Penelope: I don't think either Jeremiah or I could fly.

Homer: Why not?

Penelope: Mother always taught us to stick close to each other.

Homer: We've always been close to each other, and we'll continue being close. (He points to the monitor.) We'll watch the rocket from here all the time.

Penelope: Then why not let Sylvester fly? We can guide him from the control room.

Sylvester (proudly): Yes. I want to fly.

Homer: We need him here. The pilot must have good vision in order to control the rocket. You saw what almost happened here.

Penelope: We will not risk our lives.

Homer: There's no risk to fly in Homer 1. (He pauses, but sees no response from either Chicken. He turns to the Geese.) What about you, Prunella, … or you, Bartholomew?

Prunella: We, too, don't want to risk our lives. Our mother would be sad.

> Homer seems nervous. He paces the room, thinking, then approaches Sylvester.

Homer (sighing): I'd love to have your vision suddenly come back to you. I know you are brave, courageous, and quite able; but we need someone with good vision.

Sylvester: My vision is not as important to me as my courage and determination. I know I can do it. I'm confident I can handle the mission successfully. Don't let a little thing like my vision be an obstacle. I want to fly!

Homer looks at the wall clock again.

Homer (nervously): We really don't have a lot of time left. We have to launch the rocket on schedule. We have to decide right now who will fly — one of the four of you. (He points to the Chickens and Geese.)

Sylvester (to Homer): You're just wasting your time, my dear Homer, trying to persuade one of your reluctant crew to take off into space. I'm the only one on this team who wants to fly. Let me do it!

He makes a move toward the control table.

Homer (shouting): Stop right there! You're already too close to the control table.

Sylvester steps back until he touches the wall.

Sylvester (begging): I can see everything in my mind's eye. I have a plan to guide Homer 1 to the planets.

The others laugh at Sylvester.

Sylvester (annoyed): Don't laugh at me. (He pauses a moment, deep in thought.) ... I think I've got it. ... Yes, I have it! (He jumps up and down.)

Homer (with surprise): What have you got?

Sylvester is still jumping up and down with excitement. Homer gets to him and holds him still.

Sylvester: Don't touch me! (He struggles free.) I have it! I finally have it! (There is silence for a moment.) I have the courage to fly. I want to be first on another planet.

Homer: I don't want you talking about flying anymore.

Sylvester (thinking): Wait a minute. If no one will fly ... what will happen to your mission?

I WANT TO FLY

Homer: Any one of us could fly. It's our mutual dream.

Sylvester: If you really think so, why don't you let me fly?

Homer: You don't seem to understand. You are not eligible to fly.

Sylvester (sadly): If only my vision would come back to me.

> The others look at Sylvester in sympathy.

Homer (to Sylvester): My dear Sylvester, I'm sorry!

Sylvester: I want you to realize your dream. I don't want you to give up.

> Homer gets closer to the monitor and looks at the rocket for a moment. Then he turns to them.

Homer: We have to assess everyone's abilities and select the one with the best qualifications. That will determine who will pilot Homer 1. That's only logical — and fair. Don't you agree?

> They look at one another silently for a moment.

Sylvester: What does that mean?

Homer (to Sylvester): I'm sorry, you're not included. (To Penelope.) OK. You're first. Come with me to the examination room. We have a few simple tests to perform. Things like a few spin tests, flying upside down, and so on. Just the basic things that should have been performed earlier but were neglected. Come along.

> Homer enters a door with "Examination Room" written on it. Penelope follows. Sylvester leans sadly against the wall. Jeremiah, Prunella, and Bartholomew look at the rocket on the monitor.

Jeremiah (to Prunella): It would sure be scary to fly in that rocket.

Sylvester: I'm not scared of flying. I wish none of you pass the tests. I want to fly that ship. I want to explore the other planets.

Prunella (laughing): How would you see the creatures on the other planets — even if they did exist?

Sylvester (nervously): I don't have to actually see them. There are other ways of studying them than merely looking at them, you know.

> The door of the examination room opens. Penelope comes out. She seems to be dizzy. She staggers and falls to the floor. Jeremiah helps her get up.

Penelope: I can't see a thing. Everything is turning. I'm so dizzy. Ah, my head! (She turns to Jeremiah.) It's your turn, brother. I guess we Chickens aren't meant to fly.

> Jeremiah goes into the examination room.

Sylvester (excitedly): What about the Goose family?

Prunella: We're really no better off than the Chickens.

Sylvester: Then Homer has no choice but to take me. I'll be the future pilot of Homer 1.

(He begins to sing.)
No more, no less;
Everyone knows
That I'm the best.

> The door of the examination room opens. Jeremiah comes out, also reeling dizzily before he, too, falls to the floor.

Jeremiah: It's no fun to fly.

Penelope (worrying): Do you think you made it?

Jeremiah: I don't know, but I didn't like the exercises. (To Prunella.) I guess it's your turn.

> Prunella enters the examination room. Jeremiah throws up.

Sylvester: Who's that bringing up his breakfast?

Penelope (holding Jeremiah): My brother. It looks like we Chickens weren't meant to fly.

Jeremiah: I don't think anybody can make it to the Red Planet.

Sylvester: Don't say that. I can make it.

Jeremiah: I bet you can't.

Sylvester: Everyone thinks I'm handicapped. (loudly) But I'm not. I want to fly! I want to make my mark on this planet ... (He points to the sky.) ... and on that planet, too! (He begins singing again.)

My name is repeated by every mouth.
My wisdom is heard from north to south.
(He laughs.) That's my song. I will never forget it.

> The door of the examination room opens and out comes Prunella. The same thing happens to her, and she falls. Bartholomew quickly catches her.

Bartholomew: Are you all right?

Prunella: I don't feel so good. Flying is pretty dangerous.

Sylvester: I'm not afraid to take the necessary risks for the success of Homer 1.

Prunella (to Bartholomew): It took just two seconds and I was sick. I felt my stomach all mixed up. Everything was upside down. (To Bartholomew.) It's your turn. Go, and good luck. Excuse me. I've got to find the bathroom. (She rushes off.)

> Bartholomew enters the examination room, somewhat hesitantly.

Sylvester: I hope the Geese don't have any better luck either.

Jeremiah (to Sylvester): We're courageous and brave. We just don't like to take chances.

Sylvester (laughing): Why did you throw up? You couldn't even take the exercises.

Prunella: It's just not my day.

> Prunella reenters the room, still looking pale and ill.

Sylvester: We'll just have to wait and see how your brother makes out.

> Bartholomew enters. He is about to fall when Prunella catches him.

Bartholomew: It seems that everything is turning around.

Sylvester (triumphantly): Aha! Nobody made it! He'll have to take me now!

> Homer enters, obviously discouraged and frustrated. There is a moment of silence.

Homer (dejectedly): I didn't expect such negative results. (He sits.) It looks as if I'll have to fly in Homer 1.

> They all look at him silently.

Sylvester (moving nervously): Who will coordinate the mission from the space centre?

Homer: Any one of you can do it.

Sylvester: Are you giving up on your dream, then?

Homer: What do you suggest, my dear Sylvester?

Sylvester (confidently): I still believe I can make it to the Red Planet.

> Homer paces the room for several minutes, deep in thought. He moves closer to the monitor and gazes at it intently for a moment.

Homer: As I see it, we have two choices: We can launch the rocket without a pilot … or … we can let Sylvester be the pilot of Homer 1.

Sylvester (very excited): Oh, please let me fly. I'll do everything possible to make the mission succeed.

Homer (to Penelope): What do you Chickens think? Do you agree to letting Sylvester fly?

Penelope: If he has enough confidence, why not let him fly?

Homer (to Prunella): What about the Goose family?

Prunella: We're in favour of letting Sylvester fly Homer 1.

Homer (to Sylvester): I guess it's settled, then. I hope you make it back safely.

Sylvester (excitedly): Then I'm to be the pilot?

Homer: That's right! If you follow the orders you receive from the King Mortimer Space Centre … you are our pilot.

Sylvester: I most certainly will. My duty is to carry out whatever instructions Mission Control gives me. I'm ready to leave right away, if necessary.

Homer (to Jeremiah): Take Sylvester to the training room and get him ready to fly.

Sylvester: I'm ready now.

Jeremiah guides Sylvester into the training room.

Homer (to Penelope): Liftoff will be on schedule. We have to make just a few minor adjustments to make it easy and safe for Sylvester.

Penelope (smiling): A magic white cane with all the control buttons on it! (To Prunella.) Come, you will help me make this remote control cane. Let's go to the lab.

Penelope and Prunella exit. Homer and Bartholomew are still looking at the monitor. Nigel and Priscilla Pigeon appear in the monitor. Homer sees them.

Homer (surprised): Nigel and Priscilla Pigeon! What are they doing there? I want them to stay away from the rocket. (To Bartholomew.) Bring them in here, please. (Bartholomew exits. Homer resumes watching the monitor. He speaks quietly to himself.) I once dreamed about the sun! (He chuckles.) I dreamed I would fly and touch the edge of the sun! (He chuckles louder, almost derisively.) Am I a foolish Duck or what? ... No. ... I'm no fool! I just want to be the best I can be in the field of my choice.

Homer continues pacing in the control room until Bartholomew enters with Nigel and Priscilla Pigeon.

Nigel (to Homer): Everyone at the lake is waiting for the rocket to be launched.

Priscilla (with excitement): King Mortimer is very happy to see your dream finally come true. You know, he also dreamed of flying to the other planets one day.

Homer looks at the wall clock, then to the rocket on the monitor.

Homer: It's eleven o'clock. One hour to liftoff at noon.

Priscilla (questioning): I still don't understand how a blind person can fly a rocket?

Homer: No problem. Our technology has taken care of all the difficulties. We made a white cane with all the controls on it. In thirty minutes Sylvester can learn the whole system. (He checks the wall clock again.) Forty-five minutes to liftoff.

At this moment Sylvester appears on the monitor holding

a white cane with its handle full of buttons. He wears an astronaut's thick white uniform. On his left shoulder is a design showing an olive tree branch with seven leaves and seven black olives. He gets into the small automatic van, which drives him to the launch pad. Penelope, Jeremiah, and Prunella enter the control room.

Penelope (to Homer): He learned every button's function at the first demonstration.

Homer: Excellent job! (He looks at the wall clock.) Only thirty-five minutes to liftoff.

They all disperse to the various controls, getting ready to take care of their duties. Penelope watches her console display; Prunella checks the communication system; Jeremiah fine-tunes the monitor to get sharp images, and Bartholomew makes contact with Sylvester.

Bartholomew (into the microphone): Everything is set up. Liftoff is in fifteen minutes.

Sylvester gets out of the van and into the elevator. He crosses the swinging arm to reach the white room of the one-pilot spacecraft.

Penelope (to Homer): So far, so good!

Homer (into the microphone): Sylvester, is everything okay?

Sylvester's voice: Yes, sir.

Homer: Liftoff in ten minutes. (To Penelope.) Start engine number one.

Penelope: Yes, sir. Engine number one on, sir.

A plume of thick smoke billows from the rocket.

Homer: Now engine number two, please.

Penelope: Yes, sir. Engine number two on, sir.

A huge amount of smoke covers the area.

Homer (to Prunella): Release the pad.

Prunella: Pad released, sir.

The rocket in the monitor is released from the pad.

Homer (counting): 10…9…8…7…6…5…4…3…2…1… and … we have liftoff.

Homer 1 bursts into the sky, leaving behind it a huge trail of thick smoke which they all look at through the monitor.

Sylvester's voice: Congratulations! You have done a good job.

Homer (into the microphone): Have a good trip. You're on your way!

They hug one another joyfully. Nigel and Priscilla keep watching the rocket on the monitor.

Nigel (to Priscilla): Do you think Sylvester can make it to the Red Planet?

Priscilla: Maybe. … I don't know. … I think so.

The rocket continues its journey into the sky.

Sylvester's voice (over the speaker): This is Homer 1. Come in, Space Centre Control.

Prunella (into the microphone): King Mortimer Space Centre Control here.

Sylvester's voice: I don't read you. Can you read? This is Homer 1. Do you read me?

Prunella (to Homer): Homer 1 is having some difficulty with communications.

> Homer quickly gets to his desk and begins pushing buttons.

Homer (into the microphone): This is Control. Do you read us?

Sylvester's voice: It's difficult to hear you. You're breaking up. I can barely make you out.

> The rocket is seen on the monitor for a little while. Then it slowly fades as static obscures it momentarily.

Homer (to Bartholomew): The rocket is disappearing from the screen. Do something.

Bartholomew: Yes, sir. I'm trying.

Homer (into the microphone): This is King Mortimer Space Centre Control. Homer 1, do you read us? (To Bartholomew.) Clear the screen.

Bartholomew: I'm trying. I can't do anything.

Homer: We're losing contact. (To Jeremiah.) What do the weather conditions look like?

> Jeremiah checks the weather map on three different display screens.

Jeremiah: For the time being, it seems to be good, but some storms are coming from the east. I predict poor visibility shortly.

Homer (to Prunella): Are you still in contact with Sylvester?

Prunella: I can't make out anything he's saying. It's all garbled!

Homer (nervously): What's going on?

Prunella (into the microphone): This is King Mortimer Space Centre

Control. Can you read me, Sylvester? (She turns to Homer.) We've lost all contact. (She takes off her headset.) Even the tone has disappeared.

The rocket disappears completely from the monitor.

Bartholomew: What's going on? No pictures?

All look at the monitor.

Homer (sighing): We've lost all contact. What happened? We've failed! What went wrong? I thought we had every last detail planned perfectly. What went wrong? Was it human error, or mechanical failure?

They look at each other sadly. A moment of silence.

Penelope: I think it's a communications problem.

Homer: Are you saying our advanced communication system can't contact Homer 1?

Penelope: It sure looks that way.

Nigel and Priscilla Pigeon prepare to leave.

Nigel: I'm very sorry for Sylvester.

Priscilla: How can a blind person find the right buttons?

Homer: He'll figure it out. We've just lost contact with Homer 1, that's all.

Homer goes to the communications console and tries tuning in the spacecraft himself. A few squawks and squeaks come through, but nothing meaningful. Then the speakers go completely silent.

Bartholomew: I don't believe we'll get a picture from Homer 1 for a long time.

Homer paces the room. Penelope goes to help Prunella with the communication system.

Penelope: Don't give up. We may have a problem, but we'll be able to solve it.

Homer: That's what we have to do. Let's get started.

Penelope: If it's not pilot error, we will find the cause of the problem. If it's a mechanical failure, it's our fault.

Homer: It's not Sylvester's fault and it's not a mechanical failure. It's only a communications problem. The ship is working fine, I tell you.

Homer sits on the floor sadly. Penelope manipulates the console, trying to make contact with Sylvester. The squawks and squeals continue. Nigel and Priscilla Pigeon exit quietly. Suddenly the control room darkens as the lights go out.

Homer: The power is off! What happened? What's going on?

The console continues emitting its senseless noises, which seem to echo ominously in the dark control room for a while before fading to silence.

Scene Two

Lake Serenity. It's past midday. The sky is clear. The vapour trail from Homer 1 is clearly visible in the sky. King Mortimer sits on a tree branch accompanied by Queen Hortense, Mathilda Duck, Henrietta Chicken, and Lucy Goose. All look at the sky in admiration.

King Mortimer (proudly): This is a big day for us. It's a victory. A victory for everyone.

Mathilda: How long will it take Homer to get to Mars?

King Mortimer: Quite awhile, I'm afraid. It will take months, but it doesn't matter how long it takes. The important thing is that it's happening. We will be introduced to the planets. (Firmly.) We will establish ourselves as leaders in the universe.

Mathilda (proudly): How proud I am of Homer's achievement! He's a hero! He made his dream come true. All our dreams!

Henrietta: It's also Jeremiah's achievement. We Chickens have always been eager to fly, and now we've done it.

Lucy: It's an achievement for the Goose family, too. Bartholomew and Prunella have always had the courage to make things work out.

King Mortimer: It's an achievement for everyone. It's our planet's achievement. (He turns to Hortense.) I am now living my dream. Let's celebrate this event.

> King Mortimer gets up and jumps up and down. Happily, all get up and encircle King Mortimer. They sing as they dance around him.

All together (singing):
> Let them fly.
> Let them be high.
> Let them burst into the sky.

> Nigel and Priscilla Pigeon appear flying overhead, looking for a spot to land.

Nigel (calling): My lord! King Mortimer!

Priscilla (to Nigel): It's too bad that we have to interrupt their fun.

Nigel: We have to tell them the truth.

> King Mortimer sings joyfully, paying no attention to Nigel and Priscilla.

All together (singing):
> Our dreams are added to theirs.
> We first paved the path for the new generation
> to think fast.
> Let them go! Let them go!
> The universe is vast.

> They are interrupted by Nigel. They stop singing.

Nigel (calling): My King, my King!

King Mortimer (glancing upward at Nigel): Nigel! Come share the joy of our success with us.

> Nigel and Priscilla land on the branch.

Mathilda (to Nigel): My son made it. Did you tell him I love him?

Henrietta (to Nigel): Did my children fly together?

Lucy (to Nigel): What do you have to tell about my children?

> Nigel approaches King Mortimer and whispers in his ear.

King Mortimer (surprised): What?

Nigel: I'm sorry for interrupting your merrymaking.

King Mortimer: Who finally flew in the rocket?

Nigel: It was Sylvester.

King Mortimer: What? Sylvester is guiding the aircraft?

> They all look at the sky silently. The vapour trail is disintegrating.

Nigel: No one else had the physical conditioning to fly except Sylvester.

King Mortimer (sighing): How could a blind pilot guide an aircraft in space? It's bound to be a failure. There could be an explosion aboard! Anything could happen.

Lucy (sighing): Thank God my children didn't fly.

Henrietta (worrying): I'm certainly glad my children are still on the ground.

Mathilda: I feel sorry for Homer and Sylvester. I don't want their dream to be just a dream. I still believe that Homer's dream will come true some day.

> King Mortimer sits on the branch and looks at the sky. All sit around him silently.

King Mortimer (taking a deep breath): I, too, believe Homer will make his dream become a reality here on this planet.

> They look at the sun. The lake's surface is calm. The water glitters. Sounds of birds are heard echoing in the forest; slowly the light of the sun decreases until the dark sky becomes a sea of twinkling stars.

ACT TWO
Scene One

King Mortimer Space Centre control room. Ten months have passed since the rocket ship blasted off into space. It is night. The sky is covered with thick dark clouds. The wind blows strongly. The rain is coming down heavily. The control room is dim and quiet. The monitor is on, but no picture is seen. The other monitors and the communication system are making queer crackling and whistling noises. The rain hammers against the windows, while the wind continues its relentless howling. Homer, sitting in front of a television monitor, is very tired. Penelope is sleeping on her desk. Jeremiah is leaning on the wall, deep in thought. Bartholomew and Prunella are asleep side by side on the floor. The wind picks up, and distant thunder can be heard getting closer. Lightning flashes, immediately followed by a strong crack of thunder. The rain gets even more intense. Suddenly the power goes out, leaving the control room in darkness, with just a small red emergency light still on. Voices can be heard in the darkness.

Homer (loudly): What's going on here? Why does it seem that even nature has conspired against us? We are not giving up. We'll do everything we can to get our mission accomplished. (Calling.) Penelope! Where are you? Penelope!

    Penelope wakes with a start.

Penelope (frightened): It's so dark in here. Turn the lights on. (She calls.) Homer, where are you?

Homer: I'm here, Penelope. Just listen to that storm!

Penelope: Yes, Homer. I hear it. It's a big storm.

Homer: That's why there's no light, my dear Penelope.

Penelope: I'm scared and tired, Homer; and it's only getting worse! I'm not sure I can be part of this team any longer. I'm going back to Lake Serenity.

Homer (with surprise): What are you talking about?

> Just then, a loud clap of thunder shakes the control room. There is a sound of objects like bookcases or chairs falling to the floor. Homer loses his balance and falls. Bartholomew and Prunella wake up screaming.

Bartholomew (frightened): What's going on? What's happened? Is it an earthquake? I want to get out of here.

Prunella: Just calm down. It's just bad weather. (She looks around.) Is everybody all right? (She calls out.) Homer? Where are you?

Homer (painfully): I'm here on the floor, but I'm all right. How's everybody else? Just remain in your places until the storm passes.

Bartholomew: I want to go to Lake Serenity. I want to see Mother!

Homer: My dear Bartholomew, you are not alone here. We are still a team. Together we can overcome anything that gets in the way of our ultimate achievement.

> Strong thunder rolls across the sky, rattling the windows again. The room shakes. There is the sound of more furniture moving around and falling.

Jeremiah: I'm scared, too. I want to go to Lake Serenity. I can't take it here anymore. We have spent ten months trying to get in touch with Sylvester with no success. It's just a dream to think that we'll find him somewhere in space.

Homer: We have to keep on trying. It's our duty to find Homer 1. I haven't lost hope of finding Sylvester alive.

Jeremiah (laughing): Alive? After ten months?

Homer: He has everything he needs to stay alive for fifteen months. It's been only ten months so far. We are still on schedule. There's nothing to worry about. We have to keep trying to contact Homer 1.

Jeremiah (desperately): Well, I'm giving up because we're at the end of our resources. We've tried everything we know of, and still we can't raise Homer 1. There's no hope. I'm going back to Lake Serenity. (He looks around for Penelope.) Penelope! Are you coming with me? Penelope! Where are you?

Penelope: I'm here. I can't see a thing. I think we've all become blind like Sylvester.

Jeremiah: We should leave this place right now.

Penelope: Shouldn't we wait at least until the lights come back on?

Jeremiah: I can't wait any longer. I'm tired of this space centre. We have to leave before it collapses on our heads.

Penelope: It's so dark in here, and outside, too. Let's wait until it gets lighter.

Homer (angrily): Nobody is leaving the centre. We're a team! We're in this together!

Jeremiah: I don't want to waste any more of my time on a hopeless cause.

Homer: Don't be silly, Jeremiah. We have accomplished many things. We are about to see our greatest achievement. We are a good team.

Jeremiah (angrily): I told you, I can no longer be a member of this team. My sister and I are leaving.

Homer (calmly): Jeremiah, you can't leave. You are a part of this team.

Jeremiah: You heard me, Homer. We're leaving. (Calling to Penelope.) Penelope, are you ready?

Penelope: But it's so dark. I can't see a thing!

Jeremiah: Penelope! Come toward my voice. Can you hear me? I'm here beside the communications console. Come. Walk toward my voice.

Penelope: I'm scared to touch something that could ruin everything.

Homer: Penelope! Don't move. Don't listen to Jeremiah.

Jeremiah: Penelope! We are brother and sister. We've done everything together.

Penelope: Yes, we have.

Homer: But we are teammates. We are more than brother and sister; we are partners.

Prunella (calling): Bartholomew! … Bartholomew! Can you hear me?

Bartholomew: Yes, I hear you, but I can't move my legs. Something is holding them down. I seem to be stuck.

Prunella: Do you need help?

Bartholomew: No, I think I can make it. I'm just waiting for the lights to come back on so I can see what I'm doing.

Prunella: If Jeremiah and Penelope are leaving, we should leave with them.

There is the sound of footsteps moving in the darkness.

Homer (shouting): Nobody leaves the space centre. If you do, you'll be traitors.

Bartholomew (obviously in some pain): Oh, my leg. I'm stuck. I can't move!

Homer (loudly): Don't move. Wait until the lights come back on.

> The lights flicker a moment, then the room brightens as they come on one at a time. The communication system gives out a crackling sound, followed by a series of beeping noises.

Prunella (surprised): Listen! Do you hear that? (There is a pause. More beeping sounds are heard.) It's a signal! We've made contact with Homer 1!

Homer (excited): I told you that we would get in touch with Homer 1. (He barks out orders.) Bartholomew, send Homer 1 our coordinates. Give Sylvester directions on how to get back here. Prunella, get to your monitors. Get pictures of Homer 1 on the screen.

> Prunella goes to her console, pressing buttons and switches. Bartholomew frees himself from the table that had pinned his legs and goes to his console.

Prunella (excitedly): I'm getting some pictures now!

> Homer goes to Prunella to help her with her console.

Homer: There's a picture, all right. It's getting clearer.

> The screen is still unclear, with noisy background sound.

Prunella: I hear the sound of a rocket, but it doesn't sound like ours. Could it be an alien?

Homer (with excitement): I don't think so. Our communication system is unique. If we make any kind of contact, it will be with Homer 1.

Prunella: I hope you're right!

> Bartholomew, watching the main monitor, begins to fidget.

Bartholomew (nervously): There's something queer going on. What the heck is it?

Homer rushes over to Bartholomew.

Homer: What is it? Do you have contact?

Bartholomew manipulates the monitor's controls, ignoring Homer.

Bartholomew: Here we go.

Homer (yelling): What's going on?

Bartholomew: Drat! It's gone again.

Homer (calmly): Did you contact Homer 1?

Prunella (monitoring the communication system, suddenly jumps up with excitement. She speaks into her microphone): Yes, this is King Mortimer Space Centre Control. Hello, Homer 1. Homer 1, do you read?

All rush to surround Prunella.

Homer (to Prunella): Is it Sylvester?

Prunella: I don't know! I lost him again.

Homer takes the headset from Prunella and puts it on.

Homer (into the microphone): Hello! Hello, Homer 1! Homer 1, this is King Mortimer Space Centre Control. Good morning, Homer 1.

After a few moments of silence, he takes off the headset dejectedly.

Prunella: It was him. It was Sylvester. I'm sure it was Homer 1.

Another strong peal of thunder shakes the control room. The power goes out again.

Homer (sighing): I said it before, and I'll say it again: Nothing will stop us from achieving our goal! We will fight for our existence if necessary. I believe Homer 1 is close to Earth; but for some reason, Mother Nature won't give up her fight against us. Well, we won't give up, either.

Penelope: According to our schedule, Homer 1 comes back to earth tomorrow. Is everything ready for touchdown?

Homer: That's flight operation's responsibility. (To Jeremiah.) Are all systems set for the return of Homer 1 tomorrow?

Jeremiah (laughing): What does it matter whether I'm ready or not?

Homer: This no joking matter, my dear Jeremiah. You have to be ready for tomorrow.

Jeremiah: You're just dreaming, Homer! Nothing's going to happen tomorrow. The rocket has probably blown up in some ocean.

Homer: My fellow Jeremiah, I'm the leader of this team, and I won't allow anyone to discourage our project. Get back to your duties, and don't give up hope. When the power comes back on again, we'll see what we can do next.

> There is complete silence in the control room. Only the sounds of the wind and rain can be heard. The sounds fade out slowly.

Scene Two

Exterior of the King Mortimer Space Centre. It's morning. The sky is clear. The sun has already risen above the hills. King Mortimer, Queen Hortense, Mathilda Duck, Henrietta Chicken, and Lucy Goose have just arrived. They seem surprised. They look at the space centre in awe.

King Mortimer (amazed): How could they have built this huge space centre so quickly? Where is my castle?

Queen Hortense: It's so nice to see ugly old relics transformed into beautiful objets d'art.

King Mortimer (shocked): What do you mean by that?

Queen Hortense: I often wondered how to change the empty castle of Barnyardia into a full, lively place. Now I'm glad the youngsters did it.

King Mortimer: You thought the Castle of Barnyardia was an empty place?

Queen Hortense: That was how I often felt, yes! Now I don't have that feeling anymore. I'm proud of young Homer Duck!

They gaze at the King Mortimer Space Centre with admiration. King Mortimer gets closer to a sign that says, "King Mortimer Space Centre."

King Mortimer (reading proudly): King Mortimer Space Centre. (He chuckles smugly.) That sure makes me proud of my name. I want to see what the youngsters have done so far. I want to see Homer 1 return from its mission. I feel very confident of our younger generation. (He turns to Hortense.) Let's go inside and see what this space centre looks like from inside.

All walk together to the entrance of the control room of the space centre.

Scene Three

Inside the control room, the main monitor is on. Unclear pictures come and go, and Prunella keeps trying to clear the screen using different buttons. Homer, Penelope, Jeremiah, and Bartholomew watch the screen nervously.

Homer (to Prunella): Keep working on the sound first. The pictures will come later.

Prunella: I want to identify the shape of the rocket first. Maybe it's not Homer 1.

Homer: We can identify Sylvester's voice. He speaks our language.

Prunella: More than half the earth's population speaks our language. I still want to see the picture on the screen first.

Homer: It takes so long to get clear pictures, especially if the sky is covered in thick clouds. (He gives an order to Penelope.) Get us the latest weather report!

> Penelope goes to her desk and checks the monitors for the latest weather.

Prunella (motioning for quiet): Hush! I hear something! It's a voice. I think it's a live voice.

Homer (with excitement): What did it say?

Prunella: I don't know. I couldn't understand the language.

Penelope (to Homer): The weather is clear for the time being, but the weather map shows some thick clouds coming that will soon cover the sky for the rest of the day.

Homer: We'll have to add an extra day to the schedule to avoid the bad weather.

Penelope (to Homer): That's a good idea. I see low clouds moving into our area.

Homer (to Prunella): Tell Sylvester he'll have to stay another day due to poor weather.

Prunella is still unsuccessful at getting any response.

Prunella: I'm not sure yet if it's a voice I'm hearing or just sounds of the thunderstorm.

Homer: Just keep trying to clear up the sound.

Prunella: What's going on here? It's such a strange sound.

Homer (to Prunella): A voice or a sound?

Prunella (desperately): I don't know! ... Oh! ... It's gone again.

Homer: Don't give up.

Prunella (nervously): Why don't you let me get the picture first? There are so many voices and sounds mixed together in space.

Homer: Try anything that you think is easy.

Prunella: Nothing is easy, but I want to get the picture first.

Prunella busies herself at the controls of the main monitor. Fuzzy pictures come and go for a while. Then the screen clears up and the rocket comes into view.

Homer (loudly): Look! Look at it! It's Homer 1!

A close-up of the rocket shows "Homer 1" clearly marked. They hug one another joyfully. Just then, King Mortimer, Queen Hortense, Mathilda Duck, Lucy Goose, and Henrietta

Chicken enter the control room. They stare at the group silently for a few moments.

King Mortimer (quietly): My dream come true.

Homer (to King Mortimer): We made it. He made it back. Sylvester the Blind is our hero!

They all look at the main monitor. The interior of the rocket, in close-up, shows Sylvester sleeping comfortably.

Homer: It's Sylvester! Look at him. He's sleeping! (To Bartholomew.) You have to wake him up and give him the weather conditions.

Bartholomew wears a headset and attempts to contact the spacecraft while the others watch the monitor.

Bartholomew (into the microphone): Homer 1 ... Homer 1. Come in, Homer 1. This is King Mortimer Space Centre Control.

Inside the rocket, Sylvester is stirring.

Homer: He's waking up!

They look at the monitor. Sylvester opens his eyes.

Bartholomew (into the microphone): Homer 1, this is King Mortimer Space Centre Control. Good morning, Sylvester!

Sylvester opens his eyes widely and stretches.

Homer (amazed): Look at his eyes!

They look at the monitor silently, watching Sylvester with awe.

Sylvester's voice: This is Homer 1. Do you read me? I'm coming back to earth. I'm on schedule. (Silence in the control room.) This is Homer 1. Do you read me? Come in, King Mortimer Space Centre Control. Today is my scheduled landing day. Clear me for touchdown in six hours.

Homer takes the headset and speaks to Sylvester.

Homer: Hello, Sylvester.

Sylvester's voice: Good morning!

Homer: Good morning, Sylvester. How was your mission?

Sylvester: Excellent. Everything right on schedule.

Homer: Where is your cane?

Sylvester's voice: What cane are you talking about?

Homer: I'm talking about the remote control cane we made for you.

Sylvester's voice (laughing): I don't need the cane anymore. I can see perfectly well with my own eyes, thanks to the great hospitality and care I received from the creatures I met on a distant planet six months ago.

Homer: What do you mean?

Sylvester's voice: I'll tell you everything when I land. Am I cleared for touchdown?

Homer (nervously): No, that's not possible. You'll have to stay up one more day because of the bad weather we're experiencing here.

Sylvester's voice: I'll gladly stay up one more day, and I will enjoy every second of it. See you tomorrow, then.

They look at each other silently for a while. Homer turns to the young ground crew with a big smile.

Homer (softly): He made it. … (His voice cracks and he pauses.) … Thanks to you, we made it, also. We achieved our dream. We are all astronauts. I believe we may have discovered another civilization on some other planet, if I understand Sylvester correctly. We will have to work hard to secure our future.

King Mortimer (quietly): That's certainly true, and there's no doubt that there are other creatures alive in this universe. Who knows — maybe some of them have been visiting us recently, too.

THE END

WATCH FOR OUR SPECIAL OFFER OF A FREE

T-SHIRT

with every purchase of

the four-part package of

I Want to Fly!

Part I: A Duckling's Dream

Part II: Against the Odds

Part III: Journey through Space

Part IV: A New Beginning

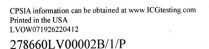

CPSIA information can be obtained at www.ICGtesting.com
Printed in the USA
LVOW071926220412

278660LV00002B/1/P

9 781432 780074